Christmas is comi

C000018256

It's time to head back t
novella...

The town is preparing to celebrate the holidays when a snowstorm hits and threatens to ruin the festivities. But that's not the only threat blowing into town...Pop's son is here from California to enjoy Christmas with his father, but when he leaves, he's taking Pop with him...or is he? Will the town give up the Godfather of Magdalena, or will they show Pop's son that when we open our hearts, anything is possible...even second chances?

Copyright 2014 by Mary Campisi

A Family Affair: Christmas is a work of fiction. Names, characters, and situations are all products of the author's imagination and any resemblance to real persons, locales, or events, are purely coincidental. This e-book is copyright protected. If you're reading this book and did not purchase it, or it was not purchased for your use, then please purchase your own copy. Thank you for respecting the hard work of this author.

PRINT ISBN: 978-1-942158-01-1

A Family Affair: Christmas

a novella

Truth in Lies, Book Five

by

Mary Campisi

Dedication:

This book is dedicated to Charlene, a woman of great talent, compassion, and kindness. There will never be another friend like you. Thank you.

Who's Who in A Family Affair: Christmas

Pop Benito: *The Godfather of Magdalena, member of The Bleeding Hearts Society, town matchmaker, dispenser of wisdom and common sense, superb pizzelle maker*

Anthony Benito: *Son of Pop and the late Lucinda Benito, lives in California, has a daughter, Lucy*

Lucinda Benito: *Pop's deceased wife, granddaughter Lucy named after her*

Lucy Benito: *Pregnant daughter of Anthony and granddaughter of Pop, currently residing in Magdalena*

Rosalyn Benito: *Anthony Benito's ex-wife and Lucy's mother*

Mimi Pendergrass: *Mayor of Magdalena, president of The Bleeding Hearts Society, proprietor of Heart Sent Bed and Breakfast, widow, lost a son, Paul, and is estranged from daughter*

Harry Blacksworth: *Former playboy turned husband and father, married to Greta, has two stepchildren and a baby (Jackson), he's Charles's brother and Christine's uncle (or is he?)*

Greta Servensen Blacksworth: *Former cook for Charles and Gloria Blacksworth, now married to Harry, mother of three children*

AJ & Lizzie Servensen: *Greta's children, Harry's stepchildren*

Jackson Blacksworth: *Harry and Greta's son*

Gloria Blacksworth: *Deceased widow of Charles Blacksworth, mother of Christine, and a woman bent on destroying her husband's "other" family...one way or another*

Nate Desantro: *A man of strength and principle, married to Christine Blacksworth, brother to Lily and son of Miriam. Runs ND Manufacturing, and has a furniture building business with Cash*

Christine Desantro: *Charles and Gloria Blacksworth's daughter, married to Nate Desantro, is a financial advisor, has daughter, Anna*

Anna Desantro: *Nate and Christine's daughter, named after Nate's sister who died hours after birth*

Lily Desantro: *Daughter of Charles Blacksworth and Miriam Desantro, half sister to Nate and Christine, has Down syndrome, is the "light" of Magdalena*

Miriam Desantro: *Charles Blacksworth's mistress, Nate and Lily's mother, artist/woodworker*

Jack Finnegan: *Plant manager at ND Manufacturing, works for Nate, worked for Nate's father*

Ben Reed: *Policeman from Philadelphia, partnered with Cash, best man at Cash's wedding*

Gina Reed: *Married to Ben and pregnant with first child. Physical therapist, friends with Tess, Bree, and Christine*

Paige Reed: *Ben Reed's cousin, a dancer who lives in Philly and once "dated" Cash*

Daniel "Cash" Casherdon: *Former policeman, married to Tess, works with Nate in furniture business and has camp with wife to help troubled kids*

Tess Casherdon: *Married to her true love, Cash, after years of separation due to tragedy. (He shot her kid brother while on duty.) Might not be able to have children; dog named Henry*

Ramona Casherdon: *Cash's aunt, raised him since he*

was eight, keeps to herself

Will Carrick: *Former police chief, widower, uncle to Tess, mentor to Cash, married to Olivia Carrick, his sister-in-law*

Olivia Carrick: *Married to Will Carrick, mother of Tess, lost son in shooting incident that tore Tess and Cash apart, estranged from older daughter*

Bree Kinkaid: *Married to Brody, friends with Tess, Gina, and Christine. Lifelong goal is to be a wife and mother*

Brody Kinkaid: *Married to Bree, works for Bree's dad, more brawn than brains, on a mission to increase his "brood" and have a son*

Rex & Kathleen MacGregor: *Bree's parents, Rex owns MacGregor's Cabinets*

Rudy Dean: *Police Chief of Magdalena, father to Jeremy*

Jeremy Ross Dean: *former junior policeman in Magdalena, now a chef, waiting for Harry's Folly to open where he'll be working*

Natalie Servetti: *Magdalena's "sleep-around" woman, and Gina's cousin*

Carmen & Marie Servetti: *Gina's parents; they believe good looks trump intelligence and integrity*

Chapter 1

For weeks, people talked about the storm that would hit Magdalena right before Christmas. They said it was going to be the worst in history, even worse than the one in '75 when the roof on St. Gertrude's church collapsed and Father Reisanski had to hold Mass at the high school until the snow stopped and the roof could be repaired.

Pop had lived through the storm of '75 and he'd live through this storm, too. Mother Nature had a way of making a person sit up and rethink his position on just what he could and could not change, like a person's attitude or destiny. There was another storm rolling in and it would be here a heck of a lot sooner. Pop squinted at his watch. Yup, the storm should be here in less than two hours, filled with gusts of hot air and enough highfalutin attitude to fill a compost bin.

That storm was Pop's son, Tony.

The boy called two weeks ago, said he was on his way back from a business trip in Virginia and planned to spend a few days in Magdalena before heading home to San Diego. Pop had enough information to load his BB gun and shoot holes in his son's story, but he let the boy talk, pretending he didn't know Tony intended to drag Pop back to California with him. Oh, but he knew all about it, starting with Miriam Desantro's phone call to his son, telling him Pop thought someone was stealing his pizzelles. The young folk believed anybody over sixty-five must have Alzheimer's if they made a claim that couldn't be supported by fact in ten seconds or less.

Well. He'd certainly supported his claim with facts. Lots of them. She had a name, too. Lucy Benito, his granddaughter. She was the one who'd been hiding out in his spare bedroom and stealing his pizzelles. Miriam couldn't apologize enough when she learned the truth and that made her the perfect accomplice to Pop's plan.

Oh, but he couldn't wait to reel Tony in.

***

Miriam added the flour mixture to the glass bowl, scraping the sides as she blended the ingredients with her hand mixer. Greta had told her that Harry ordered two more stand mixers for the Christmas baking event, but Miriam had no use for such high-end contraptions. Her hand-held mixer had never failed her, not when she'd made Charlie's birthday cakes or Lily's favorite chocolate chip cookies. Not even when she'd made fifteen banana breads for St. Gertrude's bake sale last year. There was something to be said for comfort and Greta Blacksworth seemed to understand that, because she didn't push Miriam toward the red or silver stand mixers.

If Miriam had her druthers, she'd be in her own kitchen right now, instead of Harry and Greta Blacksworth's gigantic, stainless steel one with more appliances than a service center store. But Pop had asked her to coordinate a baking event with a few of the women in town—he provided the names—so his granddaughter could learn how to make Christmas goodies from some of the best bakers in town. It wasn't like she could ignore or refuse his request, not after the horrible error in judgment she'd made: the one that had disturbed her son and hurt Pop's feelings. But how on earth was she to know that the reason behind the missing pizzelles had nothing to do with Alzheimer concerns, and everything to do with Pop's pregnant granddaughter? Oh, but she'd created a catastrophe and Pop wasn't going to let her forget about it anytime soon, which was what landed her in the same kitchen as Ramona Casherdon, a woman who'd always been a mystery and not a particularly likeable one.

"Mrs. Desantro, twenty minutes is up. Should I take the sugar cookie dough from the fridge?"

Miriam smiled at the young girl and turned off the mixer. "Of course, dear. Grab it and we'll roll it out while this one chills for a bit." Poor thing hadn't ventured toward the other end of the large granite island where Ramona Casherdon rolled peanut blossoms since the woman told her she didn't need help and preferred to work alone. Figures. That woman could not spit out a kind word if she had Tabasco sauce in her mouth.

Lucy Benito opened the stainless steel fridge and lifted out the cookie dough wrapped in wax paper. "My grandma used to make sugar cookies," she said. "She let me decorate them with colored frosting and sprinkles."

No mention of *mother-daughter* baking time. As a matter of fact, there'd been no mention of a mother at all. The town had only gotten a peek of Rosalyn Benito and that was at her mother-in-law's funeral. But that had been more than enough. "Your grandma was a great baker," Miriam said as she handed Lucy the dough for the fridge. "But your grandpa was always the pizzelle maker in the family." Miriam unwrapped the cookie dough, tore off a chunk, and placed it on the floured granite surface. "Have him teach you his tricks so you can carry on the tradition."

"I will."

Miriam caught the wistfulness in the girl's voice and recognized the loneliness in those two words, a feeling she'd known quite well at that age. It had taken years to rid herself of the loneliness, only to have it take hold again during her marriage to Nick Desantro, and not let go until she met Charlie. She guessed the poor child had a lot of emotions running through her right now. Hormones aside, what did it say about her relationship with her parents when she'd come to Pop with her troubles? Tony and his wife didn't even know their daughter wasn't still in college, let alone pregnant and living here. Oh, but that was a world of heartache waiting to happen. Since the morning Pop contacted her about Lucy three weeks ago, Miriam not only apologized for her misjudgment but agreed to help him with his granddaughter. She wasn't the only one helping the pregnant girl. Mimi Pendergrass stepped in, as well as Greta and Christine, newly married and pregnant, Gina Reed, and Tess Casherdon. Of course, Ramona Casherdon offered no help other than with the baking, but what advice would she be able to offer in regard to relationships? The town knew she'd do anything for her nephew, maybe even Cash's wife Tess, but others, for the pure sake of doing? Not likely.

Lucy Benito deserved safe haven and a chance to sort things out, and Miriam intended to help her. She looked so young, so fragile, her build small and slender with the exception of the cantaloupe-sized belly poking out from under her shirt. Her eyes were a shade lighter than "Blacksworth blue," her skin fair, her hair a mass of red curls pulled into a high ponytail. She reminded Miriam of her namesake, Lucinda Benito, Pop's dead wife and one true love.

"Mrs. Desantro, do you think Grandpa's okay?"

Miriam glanced up from the cookie dough she'd just flattened with the rolling pin. "Why do you ask?"

Lucy shrugged, darted a gaze toward Ramona. "I know I shocked him," she said, her voice low. "And he's older and older people might have weaker hearts...and if something happens to him..."

"Your grandfather is a tough man and he's not going to let a little shock take him down." Miriam squeezed the girl's hand. "He'd worry ten times more if you didn't tell him, and it's the worrying that wears a person down, not the occasional shock."

"Does the baby's father know?"

Ramona Casherdon hadn't spoken three complete sentences since she got here and now she'd asked the one question everyone wanted to know but didn't want to ask. Leave it to Ramona.

Lucy cleared her throat and said, "Excuse me?"

Ramona's dark eyes turned darker, her frown more intense. "The question is simple enough; the answer should be, too. Does the father know he's going to be a father?"

Miriam shot her a look. "I don't think that's any of our business."

"Of course it is." The woman set down her spatula and knife and made her way toward Lucy. She'd been known to intimidate the fiercest opponent, and Lucy Benito was no match for her bold questions. Miriam, however, was.

"She's not going to answer, Ramona, so don't press her. Lucy's come to Magdalena for her grandfather's help, and for a safe place to think and decide what to do. I'm going to help her, too, and I'm not the only one."

"Running from answers never solves anything." Ramona placed her hands on the counter, cocked a dark brow, and studied Lucy. "The questions won't go away, no matter how hard you try to ignore them. It's time to grow up, little girl. You've got a baby in your belly and another life to think about besides yours."

If Miriam were a cursing woman, she'd let out a string of curses, enough to decorate all five of Harry's Christmas trees. "Ramona, that is quite enough."

"He knows." Lucy slid a glance at Ramona and said, "And he's not interested. He said anybody could be the father—" her voice cracked and she swiped her eyes "— even though he knows that's not true."

"Force a paternity test," Ramona said in a matter-of-fact manner, as though they were talking about gathering herbs or vegetables for soup and not bodily fluids for parental identification.

Lucy shook her head. "I won't tie somebody to me because of a baby. I've had enough years of watching people make themselves and everyone around them miserable." She sniffed. "I will not become my parents."

Ramona looked away, asked in a pinched voice, "Your parents are unhappy?"

Bitterness coated Lucy's next words. "Unhappy? They haven't been *happy* since I can remember. How can they be when they're living on different continents?" She scowled. "Doesn't matter now because they're divorced."

"Divorced?" Miriam stared at the girl. "When? Does your grandfather know?" She'd talked to Anthony at least five times in the past two months and he'd never mentioned a word about a divorce, and neither had Pop.

Lucy shook her head. "It was official last month. Grandpa doesn't know and I don't how to tell him, but once Dad gets here it will all spill out. He'll find out I'm pregnant and Grandpa will find out he's divorced."

***

Anthony Benito settled back in first class and closed his eyes. The flight from Richmond to New York was just over an hour depending on weather, which at the moment was overcast with a drizzle, but promised to clear when they hit 4,000 feet. He'd made this trip almost three years ago for his mother's funeral, but life had been different then; Rosalyn had sat beside him, not exactly supportive, but present nonetheless, the gigantic diamond on her ring finger glittering "Mrs." status. But Rosalyn was gone, relegated to the category of "ex" though the ring lived on in one reincarnation or another.

He sighed, wished he did not have to make this trip, but how else was he going to get Pop on a plane when the man vowed to never step foot in California again? Just because the man fell and broke a few bones did not mean the state was cursed. Try telling that to the old man. He had his own opinions, lots of them, and nobody had ever been able to change them but his wife. Well, Anthony *would* get his father on a plane, and if he needed to use a bit of coercion and a mild sedative, that's exactly what he'd do.

Anthony had planned his escape from Magdalena since he was twelve years old and realized not everyone ate "greens" or homemade pasta. Some people, the *normal* ones, thought dandelions and mustard greens were weeds and therefore inedible. The second he left Magdalena, Anthony became one of those people. He shunned the simplicity of homemade pasta, opting instead for meat and prepared foods that had more to do with convenience and trends than health and nutrition. As years passed and he bought into organic, non-processed eating, he remained averse to peasant-style food choices that might reveal his ethnicity and meager upbringing.

More was better, in Anthony's eyes. A pricier car than the last, a grander home, a fancier wardrobe. More. And then he made a trip home when he was twenty-five because his mother's words sat on his shoulders and weighed him down with too much guilt. *I miss you; you're my baby, my only child. Come home, Anthony, please come home to see me.*

And that's when he met *her*, and for nineteen days, he saw life differently, especially his life. *All because of her.* The attraction was instant, explosive, all-consuming. It didn't matter that she was six years older with responsibilities he could never understand. Nothing mattered but being with her. They were meant to be together and when it was time to leave, he was certain she would join him; certain she would agree to let *her* responsibilities become *their* responsibilities. But she didn't. She didn't want him to stay either, even though he'd been willing to give up California for her. Instead, she'd sent him away.

And nothing had ever been the same.

Too much money, a lucrative advertising career, a powerful executive wife, and a beautiful daughter, gave him everything he thought he wanted. There were extra homes and cars, trips, and an accumulation of people from nannies to drivers, to cooks and groundskeepers. Anthony and his family needn't do anything but think of the next "want" and write a check to make it happen.

But somewhere along the way, perhaps after Lucy's second trip to Magdalena where she spent two weeks with her grandparents, expectations changed, at least where his daughter was concerned. She longed for her parents' time rather than the latest cell phone, concert ticket, or pair of shoes. And that was a problem, because Rosalyn Angelique Benito partitioned her time with the same stinginess she allotted to her calories: rigorous, strict, and unbending. That didn't make for a happy child or a healthy mother-daughter relationship, especially when the lackadaisical attempts were orchestrated from different time zones and often from different countries.

Anthony was slightly better, but most of his efforts were focused on stuffing and diversifying his portfolio and trying to find a way to lure his wife back to the same continent so they might attempt to have an actual marriage. Lucy's care fell to the hired help: the cook, the nanny, the chauffeur, the butler, the tutor, even the gardener. They all had stories, filled with families; spouses, children, parents, sisters, brothers, even pets; where they came from, who they were, what they wanted. Finely woven tales tied together by hope, love, sorrow, and forgiveness. It was here that Lucy learned about family, what the word meant, and sadly, what it did not mean.

But that was going to change. Anthony vowed on his dead mother's grave that he was going to have a relationship with his daughter, starting the moment she returned home for Christmas break. It was never too late to fix things, and he finally saw how much of his life needed fixing. Maybe it had taken the divorce to clear his head, but the real shocker had occurred when he told Rosalyn their marriage needed resuscitation and she'd told him maybe it was simply time to pull the plug. That had been the beginning of the end of a marriage that should never have been.

All because of the woman who'd refused his love and sent him away.

What did a person do when he found himself divorced, dissatisfied with his job, and practically estranged from his only child? The house, the club memberships, the seats on one board and another, they were all closing in on him, stripping him of oxygen and choice. He didn't want this life anymore, but the hell of it was, he didn't know what he wanted. He was fifty-three years old and now he had his father to worry about. What if Miriam Desantro's concerns that Pop might be showing signs of Alzheimer's were true? What was he supposed to do with *that?* There would be specialists to see and test after test, possibly medication, and maybe a live-in nurse. But what if he had to put him in a home? What then?

There were too many unknowns and Anthony didn't function well with uncertainty. Still, what was he to do? He wished he weren't an only child, wished he could turn to someone who understood and might help with the decisions and the responsibility. But he was it, so the sooner he got Pop to California and got the testing underway, the better. He heaved a sigh and checked his watch. In a few days he and Pop would be in San Diego waiting for Lucy to get home so they could celebrate their very own Christmas, maybe the last one Pop would remember.

Chapter 2

Rumors swirled with the snow that started two days ago, thick, heavy, spreading through town, up driveways and sidewalks, landing on doorsteps.

Guess who's coming to town? Mr. Big Shot Himself.

Well, la-di-da. Let's pull out the fancy silverware. How will I ever know which fork to use?

Why is he gracing us with his presence?

No idea. Maybe he found out about his daughter.

It's gonna be interesting.

Yup. It might be Christmas, but you can bet there'll be some serious fireworks going on.

Oh, indeed. And Pop's gonna be the one setting them off. Just you wait and see.

Hope Mr. Big Shot brought his boots. If this snow keeps up, he'll be here for a while.

Imagine that? Anthony Benito stuck in Magdalena.

The stories went on, each more inflated than the last, until word had it Pop's son planned to fly in aboard his own private jet with an entourage of staff and friends.

Harry heard all of the tales, grew more curious as the days passed and Anthony Benito's arrival grew closer. What the hell kind of joker was this guy anyway? Pop said his son was a big advertising executive and that's how Pop got all the designer sporting-wear duds and high-topped tennis shoes. There might have been some truth to that, but Harry wanted to know the rest of it, like the part the old man wasn't saying. Why had the guy stayed away for so many years? Did he think he was too good for the likes of this town? Did he want to pretend that part of his life didn't exist? If that last were true, then Harry was pissed and, given a second or two, he'd set the guy straight.

And hell, what about the poor pregnant granddaughter, Lucy? She was the guy's daughter and he had no clue. Harry shook his head and cursed. Now that was a damn shame and the situation had been laid square on Pop's doorstep. Talk about getting gray *and* losing your hair. That was some seriously screwed-up family dynamics.

Greta liked the girl and Harry liked her, too, when she worked up the nerve to talk to him. Just because he was loud, okay, boisterous, did not mean he was scary. Lizzie wasn't afraid of him; neither were any of her friends. He'd have to make it a point to get Lucy to relax around him, but how? He couldn't tell silly jokes or make faces like he did with Lizzie's friends. And offering to show her how to putt like he did with AJ was just plain ridiculous. Maybe he should sit down and have a conversation with her. What would that look like?

I see you're going to have a baby. Huh, how about that?

Or, *Damn tough luck on the kid.*

Is the father going to help out?

What's he have to say about it?

Does he know?

Do you know who the father is?

And then, *How could you do this? How?*

Now what? Damn it, now what?

Maybe he wouldn't have a conversation after all. When he looked at the girl too long, he thought of the girlfriend he got pregnant and how his parents "took care of it." Would Lucy's father try to do the same? The guy didn't seem like the type who would want his daughter labeled with an unwanted pregnancy or the status of single parent.

"Harry, why the angry face?" Greta set a glass of seltzer water with lime in front of him and sat at the kitchen table.

"Do you think parents screw up their kids?"

She sighed and placed a hand on his arm. "Harry, what is it this time? Are you still punishing yourself because you told Lizzie a scary story that made her cry?"

"It's not that." He'd forgotten about Lizzie and her crying brigade, all caused by him and his thoughtless tale of a one-legged ghost who haunted children. It was a ridiculous story, one he believed would make her laugh, not sob with hysterics.

"Well?" Her blue eyes glistened with patience.

Greta knew he was a pathetic excuse for a parent, but she never gave up on him. Actually, she gave him hope, telling him he was someone they could always count on, and in this world that was a rare gift. Maybe she had a point. He sipped his seltzer water, thought about it. Hell, yes, they could count on him. No doubt about that. So, maybe he needed a bit more polish in areas like bedtime stories. Greta could teach him that, but the other? Well, either you were a stand-up guy or you weren't.

And he'd lay a thousand bucks on this kitchen table that Anthony Benito was not a stand-up guy. "It's the girl." He shook his head, met his wife's gaze, and let her see the confusion and turmoil in his eyes. "When her old man shows up, he's going to want to take charge and then what? He'll screw with her head, start spouting off things like responsibility, duty, and how she's not ready for a kid and she might be tempted to do something foolish."

"Harry." Her voice covered him, soothed his agitation. "Look how everyone has come together to help Lucy and she's only been here a few weeks. Christine and Gina Reed have found her a doctor, Tess Casherdon takes her for the checkups, Nate is building a crib." Pause. "Even Lily and Lizzie have pitched in and picked out books for the baby."

"I guess. I see Miriam's making some kind of blanket."

Greta smiled. "It's called an afghan, and it's green, a good color of choice when you don't know the baby's sex."

"Right." He shook his head and muttered, "Speaking of sex, if she'd stayed away from it, we wouldn't be having this conversation."

"Harry. The child needs support, not comments like that."

"I know, I know. But damn, you just called her a child. How's she going to be a parent when she's a kid herself?" That was the real problem with this whole set-up of parent and child. There were no friggin' instructions.

"No one is born a parent. We all learn along the way."

That did not make him feel any better. "Yeah, so are you saying firstborns are practice for the rest? And what if there's only one? No chance to fix your screw-ups?"

Her lips eased into a smile. "It's a continual practice, like learning to play the piano or bake a pie."

Was she serious? "I know I'm new to this parent stuff, but I never heard kids compared to pianos or pies." Maybe Greta's mother, the Witch of Germany, told her that tidbit, probably said *schnitzels* instead of pies.

"This conversation isn't really about Lucy, is it?" That damnable blue gaze zeroed in on the truth. "This is about you and your worries for our children, and your ability to be a good parent."

Ding, ding, ding. She'd nailed it, dead center. Harry studied his seltzer water, took a sip, then another. Maybe by the time he finished the damn thing, he'd find an answer. But probably not, and if he tried, Greta wouldn't be impressed. That was one thing about his wife: she didn't like it when he tried to hide behind his bullshit. "Fine," he said. "You got me. These are our kids we're talking about, and what if we screw up? We'll ruin them." He ran a hand through his hair, sighed. "I hate having that on me."

"We're going to mess up, Harry." She clasped his hand, squeezed. "More than once, I suspect. But our choices will be made out of love." Her voice dipped, filled him with tiny shreds of hope. "And no child can ask for more than that."

***

"Hurry, Uncle Harry! We have to make angels before the snow melts."

Harry shrugged into his jacket and glanced out the window at the white stuff. There had to be a good six inches on the ground and it was still coming down. Pop said they could see a foot by morning. "The snow isn't going to melt until spring, Lily girl." He grinned at her, grabbed his cap, and said, "Or summer."

"Silly man." She stuffed one hand into a mitten, her eyes bright behind thick glasses. "It's best to make the angels when it's dark. Then you can look up at the sky and see the stars."

"And you stick out your tongue and catch the snowflakes," Lizzie added.

"Yup. They taste good, too." Lily grabbed Lizzie's hand and stood by the door waiting for Harry.

"Snowflakes don't taste like anything but water." This came from AJ who leaned against the kitchen table. He'd been tossing out all sorts of mood-dampening comments lately and Harry guessed it was the kid's attempt to act cool. Somebody probably told AJ that hanging out with your family was uncool. Yeah, whatever. Harry hadn't missed the way the boy had his eyes glued to the window and the snow. One of these days AJ would have to learn to ignore what everybody else said and listen to his gut. That would come years from now, hopefully, before fifty, which was when Harry "woke up." Until then, the boy might need a nudge or two and an excuse to ignore the "uncool" image; Harry could provide those nudges.

"Angels first," he said to Lily and Lizzie. "And then—" his gaze slid to AJ "—a snowball fight." The boy's face lit up like the Christmas tree on the deck, but Harry didn't wait for his response. He didn't need to because he'd seen it all on AJ's face. Ten minutes and the kid would join them, and one hundred bucks said he'd make an angel, too.

Lily, Lizzie, and Harry trudged hand in hand through the heavy snow and settled on an open space to the right of the deck, well behind the gated pool area. When was the last time Harry had sought out snow for the sake of enjoying it? He'd always avoided the stuff, considered it a nuisance and a delayer. It grounded planes, got cars stuck, shifted people in different and often incorrect directions. Its weight took out cable and power, made roofs leak, blocked driveways. It was a real pain in the ass.

He slid a look at the girls. They'd lifted their faces to the night sky, opened their mouths, and welcomed snowflakes on their tongue. No hurry, no pain-in-the-ass expressions, nothing but pure joy, so rich and deep it made Harry's chest ache. He wanted that feeling, wanted that rapture on *his* face, that snow on *his* tongue. He closed his eyes, tilted back his head and opened his mouth. The flakes hit his face, his nose, landed on his tongue, melting the instant they hit.

"Tastes like coconut," Lily said with a giggle. "Yum."

"And strawberries," Lizzie added. "Coconut and strawberry snowflakes. What does yours taste like, Mr. Harry?"

"Joy," he murmured. "Real joy." Harry kept his face tilted toward the sky, his mouth open, and welcomed the sensations.

"Is joy vanilla or chocolate?" This from Lizzie, who tugged on his jacket sleeve, her small voice curious.

Harry laughed and grinned at her. "It's both."

Lily giggled. "No, it's not, Uncle Harry."

"Hey, you have your flavors and I have mine. Now show me those angels," he said, before AJ came outside and heard the "joy" comments. It was one thing to show your true self to innocents like Lizzie and Lily because they didn't judge, but AJ might ask one too many questions and expect a deeper answer, one Harry couldn't put into words.

"Angel time!" Lily took giant steps until she stood in fresh snow. "Now, you lie down, look up at the sky, and spread your arms and legs, like you have wings and are flying. Watch." She stretched out on the ground, face to the sky, and moved her arms and legs back and forth. "And then you stand up—" she clambered to her feet, stepped away, and pointed "—and there's your angel."

"I want to make an angel!" Lizzie flopped on a patch of new snow and flailed her arms and legs, her giggles filling the night. "Come on, Mr. Harry. We need more angels."

Damn, if that wasn't the truth. Harry glanced at the door. He could make a fool of himself before AJ got outside, and he'd make Lily and Lizzie happy. What the hell? "I've got to find my very own spot and, Lily, don't hog all the snow." She was on her third angel, and if he let her go, the imprints would cover the yard in an hour.

"I won't," she called from several feet away. "Come over here and we'll make one, side by side."

The kid sure had rules on this make-believe crap. Harry sighed and clomped toward Lily with Lizzie close behind. When he located an area of glistening fresh snow, he knelt and lay on his back, face to the starlit sky. Sound drifted over him as the snow insulated his body and muted the noises of the outside world. He didn't hear Lily's giggles or Lizzie's questions; he heard nothing but the softness of his breath blowing in and out. Is this what peace felt like? He searched the sky, settled his gaze on the brightest star he could find, and opened his mouth to welcome the snowflakes. The worry over being a lousy parent, not deserving Greta, disappointing those who counted on him, all melted away with the snow on his tongue. It would no doubt return later, and there would be more fears, more worries, but right this very moment, there was peace. Harry moved his arms and legs slowly as Lily had shown him. He'd make a helluva large angel, though he did wonder if his angel would have horns on its head.

Harry was thinking about angels with horns when Lily plowed into his thoughts. "Say, hi to Daddy, Uncle Harry."

"Huh?" He lifted his head and stared at Lily who lay a few feet away, right hand sweeping the air.

"Wave to him, Uncle Harry." She kept her gaze fixed on the star-sprinkled sky. "Hi, Daddy. Can you see us? We're making angels like you showed me. Uncle Harry didn't know how, but I showed him. Can you see the snow? It's crunchy and it tastes so good." She giggled. "Your snow always tasted like peanut butter and jelly, but mine tastes like coconut and Lizzie's tastes like strawberries." She paused and her voice dipped. "And Uncle Harry said his tasted like joy, but I don't know what that tastes like. We're going to make lots and lots of angels because you said there weren't enough on this earth."

Harry squeezed his eyes shut to keep what felt an awful lot like damn tears from slipping out. Lily could make him choke up with a word, a look, hell, a hug could do it, and if he didn't shut it down, the tears would sprout faster than a sprinkler.

"Uncle Harry and Aunt Greta are having a big Christmas Eve party at their house. Uh-huh. Lots of people are coming. I don't think you know all of them, but you do know lots. I'm going to be there, so is Mom, and Nate and Christine." She paused, "And Anna, and Pop, and—" She paused a few seconds, then asked, "Who else is invited to your Christmas party, Uncle Harry? I want to tell Dad."

"Gina!" Lizzie shouted from a few feet away. "And her husband!"

"Right." Lily's voice filled with excitement. "Gina and Ben Reed and the baby in her belly."

Harry tried to block out the chatter, but part of him wanted to know what she found to say to Charlie. Pop talked to a dead wife, Lily talked to a dead father; did the whole town talk to dead people? Well, he knew one person who didn't. Harry Blacksworth.

"Do you know…?"

She went on as though Charlie were right beside her, as though he could hear her and answer. What the hell was that about? He wished Greta and Jackson would hurry up and get home from Miriam's. Wasn't it time to put Jackson to bed? And how long did it take to make a few pumpkin rolls? Not that he had any idea what went into making or baking a pumpkin roll other than pumpkin and cream cheese. But still, Greta and Miriam were expert bakers; they should have the routine down, shouldn't they? He glanced toward the deck. Why wasn't AJ outside? Had the kid decided to play computer games instead of enjoying a little fresh air and the opportunity to hear Lily talk to her dead father? Who would want to miss *that?*

Why was he so edgy? If Lily had a thing or two to say to Charlie, so what? Let her talk. He stared at the sky, blew out a breath, and forced his body to relax as her words covered him like new-fallen snow.

"We miss you, Daddy and we wish you were here. Uncle Harry could help you bring in the tree and we could all drink hot chocolate with tiny marshmallows. Remember how I like those?" On and on she went, telling him about the ham Greta planned to cook and the special stockings Miriam knitted for Uncle Harry's family, with loops to hang them from the fireplace. Her words blended with the night air, swirled over him, into him, pulling regret and tension from his body until all he could think of was Charlie.

I am so damn sorry, Charlie, and I will spend the rest of my life trying to make it right. Count on that. I don't deserve your forgiveness. Hell, I don't deserve the air I'm breathing, but here I am. We both know I would have been missed far less than you, and yet, you're the one who won't be at the Christmas table. Doesn't make a damn bit of sense, does it? God, but I miss you.

He blinked hard, closed his eyes, and sucked in the night air. Maybe Lily was on to something; talking to those you loved and lost like they were still here made you feel like you could put closure on some unfinished business, and maybe have a chance to get it right this time. Not a bad thought, not bad at all.

His newfound calmness lasted all of four seconds until Lily said, "Bye, Daddy. Tell Aunt Gloria I said hello."

***

Anthony parked on Main Street and stepped out of the car. He'd thought about buying a pair of snow boots, but decided against it. What was the point when he planned to fly out of here in a few days? He made his way onto the sidewalk, taking deliberate steps so he didn't slip. The last time he'd been involved with snow, he'd been on skis and that wasn't the same as dress loafers. He'd worn a ski jacket, too, not leather with minimal lining and gloves that were more about fashion than function. He stuffed his hands in his pockets and sighed. This was going to be a very long few days and he hadn't even seen his father yet.

The storefronts looked much the same as they had when he'd come for his mother's funeral, though many had decorated their windows with colored twinkle lights and garlands, one even had a waving Santa Claus in the window. Terra cotta pots stuffed with small evergreens, strung with white twinkle lights, stood beside the doors of random shops. The feel was quaint and welcoming and would capture the perfect tone for a Christmas card. He'd have to mention this to his artist friend who designed gift cards for all occasions. If the man could draw it, Anthony could sell it, because he could sell anything: cards, sporting wear, ideas, attitudes, a philosophy. He'd been spinning words for so many years he didn't even know what he believed any more.

Except that he did not want to be here and the sooner he left, the sooner he and Pop could get to California and see Lucy. The decision to take a detour and stop downtown had come as he waited for the rental car. Pop had always been able to read him better than anyone, and the second Anthony walked through the door, the old man would know his son hadn't just decided to check in on his return trip from Virginia. If his father knew how many times Anthony had flown to the East Coast to do business over the years, he'd have a whole arsenal of questions and queries, starting and ending with the most powerful: *Why couldn't you visit your mother more? She never got over missing you.* Fortunately, Pop didn't know about the trips, and he was not going to find out, because if he did, Anthony might have to give him an answer for his absence. And what would he tell him? Certainly not the truth.

I never belonged in Magdalena, Pop, not from the second I realized there was more to living than eating pasta fagioli and listening to stories about how my ancestors came over on the boat from the old country and settled in this town. What was the point of retelling those stories? Why let everyone know you were born poor when you could emerge in a city and become anyone you wanted to be? Anyone! I belonged in the city, surrounded by people with big ideas and lots of opportunity, where there was no limit to the amount of money you could make. Who wouldn't want that? And once you had it, why would you return to a place that made you feel small, that threw your accomplishments back at you and couldn't understand its own insignificance?

How could he tell his father *that* without causing irreparable damage to their relationship? It was better to lie and protect him than to tell him the truth. And then there was the other reason—*her.*

He couldn't tell his father any of it. Absolutely not. He pushed the truths from his brain and scanned the street. It was too cold and there was too damn much snow. Why would a person actually *enjoy* the stuff unless he were skiing in it or watching it on a big screen? Anything other than that was a no-thank-you. But these people didn't seem to mind. A couple emerged from Lina's Café, the Hollywood-handsome man laughing as the dark-haired pregnant woman smiled up at him. They didn't seem to notice the cold or the snow as they walked hand in hand down the street. Anthony kept his eyes on them until they disappeared into Victor's Pharmacy. Old man Winston used to run the place, and he used to yell at them for "loitering" outside, said they scared away his customers. What scared them away was his wife Zelda's mustache.

A fifty-something-year-old man in a cashmere coat and plaid scarf headed toward him, whistling as though he didn't mind the snow or the temperature. He carried two shopping bags stuffed with what looked like Christmas gifts, the wrapping and ribbons foiled and bright. He nodded at Anthony as he passed, then continued on to his car, a Jaguar. Who was the man and where was he going? And why was he in Magdalena when he had the brand of city life on him?

Did Pop know these people? Did he walk down Main Street and have conversations with the waitress and the barber, asking about their children, their grandchildren, their health conditions? What about Hollywood-handsome and his pregnant lady? And the man in the cashmere coat? Did Pop know them, too? Anthony pictured it all, foreign and yet as familiar as Victor's Pharmacy storefront. Some things never changed and that was exactly why he'd avoided this town for so many years. Part of him wanted to head into Lina's Café for a cup of coffee and a little more time to delay the inevitable confrontation. He'd never been good at tackling an issue head on; had preferred dancing around it, avoiding it, even ignoring it in hopes the situation would solve itself or simply disappear. Those tactics hadn't worked, but it hadn't stopped him from trying.

Well, today would be different. He was going to get back in his rented BMW, drive to the house where he'd grown up and where Pop would be waiting with a tray of pizzelles and ten reasons why Anthony was not dressed for Magdalena weather, and he would say what he'd come to say. Period.

Chapter 3

When Pop heard the car outside, he straightened his string tie and rolled a lint brush over the legs of his trousers. The last time he wore this suit was when he laid his beloved Lucy to rest. He'd had no need for it in all the months since, but for today's mission to be a success, a suit and tie were required. Pop tossed the lint brush in a drawer and moved to the front door to watch his son.

Tony had never been a big boy, probably didn't stand 5' 9", but when he opened that mouth and started talking, he could make you think he was eight feet tall. He was a looker with those dark eyes and that black hair, curling in waves his mother had said were wasted on a man. That boy had a smile that followed you around the room, made you want to pull up a chair and get to know him. That's why he'd been so good at his job; the boy could sell rotten cabbage and make you think it was the sweetest perfume on this green earth.

And now he was here to do the big sell on Pop.

Tony stepped out of the car, one of those foreign jobs with the fancy headlights, grabbed a small suitcase, and made his way to the sidewalk. Nate Desantro had stopped by early this morning and shoveled for Pop, but his efforts were long gone as fresh snow covered the areas. When Tony started up the steps, Pop opened the door and called out, "Tony! Welcome home."

His son glanced up, threw him a quick smile that looked more nervous than happy, and said, "Hi, Pop. Good to see you."

Again, the tone and the expression didn't match up. If Pop weren't on the hunt for these discrepancies, he might not notice them, and that would give his son the advantage. Lucky the truth of his son's plan had spilled out of Miriam Desantro's lips the second she realized Pop Benito had a valid reason for suspecting a thief was stealing his pizzelles—because it was the truth. Not only that, the thief was his granddaughter, and she was pregnant. Now if that didn't beat all, not much did.

Tony stepped inside the house where he'd been raised, looking dapper and citified and like he'd rather be eating a bowl of pasta fagioli—the boy had always hated it—than standing here right now. Pop ignored the pang in his chest and gut and opened his arms wide to hug his only son. Wrong might be wrong, and while Pop didn't agree with the boy's plan to hijack him back to California, they had bigger problems right now. Once Pop set Tony in his place, they'd talk about those issues, namely, a pregnant Lucy and a divorce his son "forgot" to mention.

"Have a seat. How about a cup of hot tea or coffee? Maybe a pizzelle or two? Come to think of it—"

"Pop. I'm fine." Tony sank into a chair in the living room, not four feet from his mother's picture that hung over the mantel, a fitting place for a son to make his confession. Pop sat in his usual chair and faced his son. "Come to take me back, haven't you?"

"What?"

Tony had never been a good liar, not when he stole cherry tomatoes from Dolly Finnegan's, and not when he told them his future bride wanted to exchange vows at some destination place, like she was sailing off on an adventure, which just so happened to be out of "travel" range for Pop and Lucy. Well, Tony had sailed off the deep end and gotten hitched to a high-society girl who didn't want to be reminded of her husband's upbringing.

"Something tells me this isn't a holiday visit, and you didn't come here because you want to sit down and chit-chat with neighbors and have a piece of nut bread. You came for your mother's funeral—" he scratched his jaw and nodded "—and the time before that...huh. When was that? Seems I can't recall, but then my memory might not be as good as it was." *Hah*, let Tony touch that one with a garden rake because Pop was waiting, ready to show him just how much his brain still synapsed.

Tony shrugged and looked away like he used to when he was a boy and his mother asked if he'd finished the homework he hadn't started. It was always a story with Tony, and Pop had a feeling this tale would be no different, stuffed with fabrication and exaggeration. Could the boy not tell the plain truth one time? Did he always have to dress it up and dab some fancy aftershave on it in order to make it more agreeable? Rotten cabbage was rotten cabbage. No matter how many times you called it perfume, the dang stuff still stunk.

"Tony?"

His son cleared his throat and dragged his gaze to Pop's. "I did come to see you," he paused, darted a glance at the picture of his mother, then back to Pop. "I thought we could have our own Christmas in San Diego, just me, you, and Lucy."

"Huh." Now they were getting somewhere. "What about Rosalyn? She too busy gallivanting all over the world pushing coats and belts to spend Christmas with her family?"

Now came the blush, creeping from his tanned neck to his cheeks. "It's women's outerwear and accessories, and it's a very important position."

"Sounds like it." Pop nodded his head and studied his

son. At fifty-three, the boy still had a lot of growing up to do, or maybe it was "facing up" to things like reality, choices. *The truth.* Denial was an ugly creature, especially when it lived in your gut and ate at your soul like a tapeworm.

Tony threw him a look and said, "You never liked her."

"Never disliked her either." That was the truth. "Your mother and I never got to know her, what with her flitting to Tokyo and London and wherever else she went instead of staying on the same continent with her family."

"Rosalyn is a global vice president, Dad. She's a busy woman."

Tony only called him "Dad" when he meant business, the kind that made him uncomfortable. "Vice president, huh? Of the United States? Because anything less than that and maybe not *even* that is no excuse for ignoring your family."

"Oh, for the love of…" Tony sighed and ran a hand through his hair. "I'm not here to talk about Rosalyn."

"Maybe you should be." *Maybe you should be owning up to the divorce.*

"What does that mean?"

Prickly, prickly. Wait until he heard about Lucy; he'd be shooting quills faster than a porcupine under attack. "Where *is* your bride? Is she changing the sheets in the spare bedroom, hoping I'll be on the plane with you when you leave?" Pop had called Lucy his bride until the day she closed her eyes for the last time. Their life hadn't always been a grand party, but they'd stuck together, no matter how deep the manure, and when he looked at her, his Lucy was as beautiful as she'd been on their wedding day.

"Rosalyn's in Tokyo." Tony sprang out of the chair and started pacing. Not like he could get too far what with the coziness of the room and all the furniture, but the boy acted like he needed to be in motion, no different from when he was nine and had a bad case of mosquito bites. He must have jumped from room to room while his mother chased him with lotions and remedies to quiet the itching.

"Hmm. Tokyo." Pop adjusted his glasses and nodded. "Tokyo," he repeated.

Tony swung around to face Pop, his mouth pulled into a flat line, his dark eyes a jumble of frustration. "And she's not my wife anymore. We're divorced."

"Hmm." Pop nodded, once, twice. "That's going around."

"That's all you have to say? I just told you I'm divorced from Lucy's mother, the woman I was married to for twenty-seven years, and you can't formulate a sentence longer than two words?"

Oh, but there was some serious agitation and anger in that voice. "I figure if I pounce on you with questions and comments, you'll close up tighter than a cherrystone clam. But if I wait and let things settle, then you might be more willing to tell me the what, the why, maybe even the how."

His son's brows pinched together like he was trying to figure out if Pop meant what he said or if he meant something else altogether. That was the problem with people like Tony; they were so busy putting a spin on every word that came out of their mouth, they got confused between what they said to get the sale and what they actually believed. And that was dang sad. Something like that could tear a person apart from the inside out, faster than two jalapeño peppers eaten straight up, seeds and all. Pop shook his head and eyeballed his son. "I'm not giving you double talk and fancy phrases you can't cut through with a ten-inch knife. Sit down and talk, or don't. Either way, I need a pizzelle." He stood, adjusted his tie, and said, "You want one?"

"No. Thanks." And then, "Why are you all dressed up?"

Pop smiled. "I like to be on my game when I'm going against my opponent."

"Me? I'm your opponent?"

"You're not much of a challenge. I could read through you like plastic wrap." He shook his head and chuckled. "I can teach you a thing or two about not showing your hand." Pop made his way to the kitchen, lifted the box filled with pizzelles from the refrigerator, and carried them into the living room. "Sure you don't want one?"

His son stared at the stacks of golden pizzelles, all lined up and ready. "Okay, I'll have one."

"'Course you will. Nobody can refuse my pizzelles." Tony still fought his upbringing and his Italian heritage, but maybe one day, he'd stop being embarrassed by it. Pop handed him one and took two for himself. "Take as many as you like. Bet they don't make them like this in California."

The truth behind Tony's divorce spilled out between bites of pizzelles and the saddest eyes Pop had seen in a long time. There hadn't been an affair, a raised hand, or a blowout. Tony and Rosalyn simply lived different lives that rarely crossed. She poured her time and energy into the company she loved and for years, as he advanced in the advertising agency, he'd been fine with that. Who didn't want more money, a fatter retirement portfolio, and enough frequent flyer miles to jaunt to Chicago and New York City for the weekend? And what about fancy cars, designer clothing, memberships to private clubs, and collections—of everything. Who wouldn't want *that?*

Two years ago, with Lucy leaving home and heading to

college, Tony realized he wanted more than a wife who lived in another part of the world, who slept in a different bed, and who didn't seem to mind that she did. Rosalyn had made a half-hearted attempt at the holidays the year Pop ventured out there, probably because Lucy was coming home from college.

But the damage had been done long ago with the silence and the separate lives. Tony shared his story with Pop, his shoulders sagging with the telling, his voice dipping lower with each memory. "Come back with me, Pop. Lucy will be home in a few days and we can do Christmas right: a tree, tinsel, ornaments." His voice rose as he spoke of decorating the tree. "Even a blinking angel on top."

Pop eyed him with a no-nonsense look and said, "You're not worried I'll forget how to string a tree, or maybe wonder why there's even a tree in the living room?"

His son stared at him. "What are you talking about?"

"Alzheimer's." *Zing!* Let the boy deny that one. "Isn't that why you're really here? You want to take me back with you and toss me in one of those old folks' homes where I can't grow basil or sit in my underwear."

"Pop. Listen." He cleared his throat, twice, tried to speak, but nothing came out.

"I'm listening, but I'm not hearing anything." Before Tony could regroup and spit out a tale coated with more sweetness than a sugarplum, Pop said, "You think the people in this town are going to let you take me away?" He snapped his fingers, ignoring the twinge of arthritis in his thumb. "Just like that? Because you're my son?"

"Miriam Desantro called me because she was concerned."

Now he was getting all huffy like he used to when he didn't get his way. Too dang bad. "Miriam Desantro made a mistake."

Tony ignored him. "I made a special point to get here as soon as I could. We need to get you checked out, make sure there's not an issue."

"Issue? If something doesn't feel right, I'll see Doc Needstrom. He'll know what to do; been practicing for almost as many years as you been walking this earth."

"That does not make me feel good. The man is ancient."

"He knows what he's doing." It was Pop's turn to get huffy. "Getting old doesn't mean getting stupid."

"I didn't say that. Miriam was worried and called me."

Pop rubbed his chin and pictured his son's expression when he learned about Lucy. Those sad eyes were going to get a lot sadder. "Hmm."

"Look, Pop, can you just work with me? I want you to go back to San Diego with me and get some testing done. That's it. If everything checks out, I'll bring you back home."

The boy couldn't look at him when he said the part about bringing him home. That was because he didn't intend to bring Pop back to Magdalena. Nope. Pop would bet two boxes of pizzelles that his son planned to keep him in California in one of those fancy places they called retirement communities. Well, that was a big no-thank-you. Tony might think he had to worry about Pop, but once he found out he was going to be a grandpa, he'd really have something to worry about. "All that bellyaching you just gave me about your marriage falling apart, were you trying to get my guard down because you thought it would make it easier to talk me into hopping on that plane?"

"Of course not."

But Pop didn't miss the darting eyes or the extra puff of air in the words. *Dang, but the boy had been trying to play him!* "Your mother would be awful sad to hear you're still fabricating to get what you want, even after all these years." He stared at his only son and said, "This is the first time since I lost her that I'm glad she's not here. It would be too painful for her to witness you trying to con your old man."

Oh, but the boy didn't like that. He gripped the arms of the flowered chair, dark eyes narrowed, and spat out, "I am not trying to con you. You know I don't like coming to this town, but I suffered this damned snow to get to you. Can you try not to be so ungrateful?"

Pop sat back in his chair, crossed his hands over his belly, and nodded. "Ungrateful. Hmm. I can try, but I'm going to protect what's mine, like my freedom and my house." He held up a hand before Tony could start yammering about how inconvenienced he was to be in Magdalena. "I'm not going to California for Christmas. I'm staying right here and you're welcome to spend it with me," he paused, added, "and Lucy."

Tony glanced at the portrait of his mother hanging over the mantel. "Pop—"

"Not your mother, your daughter."

"Lucy's coming here?"

Oh, but there was a heap of confusion on his face, thicker than molasses in a jar. "She's not coming here. Lucy *is* here."

Chapter 4

Anthony would always remember the second he learned his daughter was pregnant. His father had refused to expand on his comment that Lucy was in Magdalena, saying only that he'd see the truth soon enough. Cryptic words, coated with double meaning. When had Pop worried about trying to bury messages in his words? He'd always been a "say it like it is" kind of guy, no sugar, no toppings. But this thing with Lucy, well, that had a whole different feel about it, from the bushy, pinched brows on his father's face to the gentleness in his voice, as though he were protecting her. But from what? Something school related? Hard to imagine when she was an honors student. Health? Of course not; she was twenty years old. What then?

The "what" revealed itself moments after Lucy entered the house, her winter jacket and hat dusted with new snow, a cautious smile on her face. Tony had jumped up from his chair and made his way to his daughter, burying her in a hug. He'd never been a parent to scold and comment on choices and shortcomings, and now he almost wished he had been. Then, it would be in character for him to demand to know what she was doing at her grandfather's and why she wasn't in school, finishing exams. The best he had was a lukewarm "Imagine my surprise when your grandpa told me you were here." She'd darted a glance at Pop, who nodded twice.

It had been a signal, he realized that hours later as he dissected the event. The signal had been followed by Lucy shrugging out of her jacket, pulling off her hat, and turning toward the coatrack. As she reached to hook the jacket, her sweatshirt hugged her middle, exposing a small, yet very present ball where her once-flat stomach had been.

Lucy? Are you pregnant?

That had been the beginning of more than he wanted to hear. Yes, his only daughter was indeed pregnant, and no, the father of the baby would not be involved. Yes, she intended to stay in Magdalena until the baby was born, maybe even after, and no, she would not be returning to college.

Anthony had volumes of questions but before he got warmed up, Pop stood and announced they had a dinner invitation to Harry and Greta Blacksworth's house, whoever that was, and if they didn't get on the road this very minute, they'd be late.

And now, here they sat, in a house that would have gotten noticed in upscale areas like La Jolla or Del Mar, surrounded with enough food to last three days and feed thirty people. Lasagna, spaghetti and meatballs, plates of olives and cheese, antipasto, salad, bread. Anthony recognized Harry Blacksworth as the man he'd seen earlier today in the cashmere coat and plaid scarf carrying the bags of presents. The bigger question was who was this Harry Blacksworth guy and why was he in Magdalena? That one made no sense, none at all. Who would do that? Anthony sipped his wine, a fine merlot he recognized as high-end, and took it all in. It would be a lot easier if he had a program to refer to the cast of characters in this room.

Miriam Desantro sat next to her son, and a woman named Christine, who was married to the son and somehow related to Harry Blacksworth. The son's name was Nick or Nate or maybe it was Matt. The girl with Down syndrome sitting at a smaller table with the other children was Miriam's daughter, but Miriam's husband hadn't been the father. Who *was* the father? Did anyone know? The kids at the table with Miriam's daughter belonged to Harry Blacksworth and his wife, but the guy looked a little old to have a baby. Still, from the look of his clothes and the perennial smile buried in the tanned face, he looked like a reformed playboy. The wife was a looker, too. Greta or Gloria. Or was it Goldie?

Pop knew them all and they all knew him. They knew Lucy, too, and not only that, they knew about the baby. Even the little blond girl with the curly hair who looked like Blacksworth's wife knew about Lucy's baby. Anthony sipped his wine and considered the fact that strangers knew more about his daughter's current situation than her own parents did. How sad was that?

"Bet you had a real shocker when you got off the plane," Harry Blacksworth's mouth worked into a wide smile. "This isn't California, that's for sure."

The man was right about that. "No, it certainly isn't."

"We don't mind a little cold and snow." This from Miriam's son.

"I've never been a fan of either." Though there had been a time when he might have adjusted… Were they really going to sit here and talk about the weather? Maybe they were being polite and that's why no one mentioned Lucy's condition or her father's ignorance of it. Anthony drank more wine and tried to blot out the last few hours. Near impossible, especially with all the chatter and references about people and places he used to know, didn't know, or didn't want to know. At least no one mentioned *her*.

"Uncle Harry?" The girl, Lily, tapped him on the shoulder and whispered something in his ear. Blacksworth nodded, his expression serious, and when the girl finished, he pulled her into a bear hug and kissed her cheek.

"Thank you for reminding me, Lily." He winked at her

and turned toward the adults. "We're having a Christmas Eve get-together here. I'd hoped to have it at Harry's Folly—" he frowned and shrugged "—but we've run into a few glitches."

Whatever that meant. Anthony had no idea what the man was talking about. He'd like to corner Miriam Desantro for a few highlights and explanation, beginning with why she called him about his father's health and then changed her story. She'd certainly been avoiding him since he walked in the room. Well, he was used to that; hadn't he dealt with executives who didn't like salesmen? And Rosalyn's friends were only interested in people in the fashion industry. None of that had ever stopped him from securing meetings and getting results. Miriam would be no different. One way or another, he was going to talk to her and find out what was going on.

"I told you not to buy that place, Harry." Pop shook his head and sighed. "Told you no good would come of it; that the blasted place had a curse on it, but you wouldn't listen."

"You think everything has a curse on it," Harry said. "Poor business decisions have nothing to do with curses."

The Desantro man cleared his throat and slid a look at Harry. "It's more a string of bad luck. Five owners and five husbands dead." He saluted the table with his drink and said, "Bad luck all the way around."

Pop looked at his son and said, "Remember the old Rettinger place? Milt Rettinger died five months after it opened; slipped on a wet floor and cracked his skull. Now that was a piece of bad luck. You left shortly after Joe Hogan and his wife took it over." He shook his head and made the sign of the cross. "Joe was laying a new floor when his ticker stopped. Thirty-eight years old and three babies at home."

"I think your son does not need to hear our sad stories," Harry's wife said, her voice soft and smothered with an accent. "Harry and I have faced a few obstacles getting Harry's Folly ready for its grand opening." Her blue eyes sparkled when she smiled at her husband. "But we won't give up. We will see it opened and we will break the bad luck streak."

Pop made the sign of the cross and said, "Amen to that, Greta."

The woman's smile spread. "This is our first Christmas in Magdalena and we want to honor it by inviting family and friends to our house for Christmas Eve dinner."

Harry nodded at Anthony. "You, too, Tony."

"What? Oh, no, thank you, but I won't be here... I mean, *we* won't be here." He stumbled over the words, tried to catch his daughter's attention, but she was busy twirling a mound of spaghetti onto her fork. Anthony cleared his throat, determined to rework his meaning. "Thank you, again, but we're spending our Christmas in San Diego." Pause. "Me, Lucy, and Pop."

"No, Dad. We're not."

"Lucy." He wished she'd go back to twirling her spaghetti instead of creating enough drama for a reality TV show. "This really isn't the time to have a discussion."

She met his gaze, held it. "I was pretty clear earlier. I'm staying with Pop, here in Magdalena."

Like hell she was. "You're a pregnant, twenty-year-old child. You have no idea what you want. And Pop shouldn't be here either. He needs to open his eyes and realize he can't live alone any longer." He regretted the harshness of his words the second they left his mouth, but it was too late to yank them back. Anthony glanced around the table. Harry Blacksworth fiddled with his fork. His wife had developed a sudden fascination with a piece of red onion in her salad. Miriam Desantro studied him with an expression that said, *fool*, while her daughter-in-law dissected a meatball. Miriam's son mimicked his mother's stance, but his expression said, *fool and idiot.*

And then the Desantro man opened his mouth. "Your father and daughter want to stay here."

If Anthony didn't look at the man's eyes, he could formulate an answer, even get it out. He settled his gaze on Desantro's right cheek and said, "This is a family matter."

"And in this town, family is about more than blood." Pop stared down his son, his expression fierce, determined. "These people at this table are family, Tony. *My* family. You need to respect that."

"Anthony, I started this whole misunderstanding and I'm very sorry for that." Miriam Desantro's voice covered the table with regret. "May I speak with you in the kitchen? I think we both have a few things that need to be said."

What an understatement. He'd landed in the middle of a disaster and the woman who'd put him there was about to explain. Well, she had a hell of a lot of explaining to do, starting with why she didn't call and tell him his only daughter was in Magdalena *and* she was pregnant. Anthony pushed back his chair and stood. "That's the best idea I've heard since I got here." He glanced around the table at the curious and not-so-curious faces and said, "If you'll excuse me."

He followed Miriam into a kitchen that was the size of Pop's whole house. What was Blacksworth's story and what was he doing here? Before he left this town, Anthony would find out.

Miriam sat on a chair at the granite island and apologized again. "I really am sorry, Anthony. I didn't mean to cause such problems for you." She shook her head and the stone earrings she wore dangled against her neck. "Pop asked me not to say anything and I couldn't go against him, not after I'd misjudged his actions."

"So you hung me out to dry?" He leaned against the island and studied her. She was a good-looking woman, tall and lean with an earthy quality that made him think of fresh air and fields of wildflowers. The skin on her fingers was cracked and stained with a rust color, the nails blunt and unpolished. Rosalyn would never in ten thousand years leave the house with naked fingernails. Red, fuchsia, pink, navy, olive, even black were colors of choice, but naked? That was like asking her to walk outside without her "face" on. There were a lot of criteria his ex-wife insisted upon and deemed essential to her existence: full makeup and hair, coordinated wardrobe including shoes, no flip-flops, no sweatpants unless they were designer, and absolutely no costume jewelry. She said if a woman couldn't afford real pearls and diamonds, then she was missing out on the true beauty in life.

But Miriam Desantro didn't look as if she bought into Rosalyn's mantra, not at all. As a matter of fact, Miriam seemed the type to rebel against women like his ex-wife, opting instead for a man's watch and comfortable shoes, definitely not designer. He'd known her years ago, had kept in touch since his mother's death, calling every few months for an update on his father with the understanding she'd contact him sooner if there was a problem. The old man had passed inspection every time, fit and ready to walk another stretch of mile in the high tops and sweat outfits Anthony sent him. But then Miriam called and told him about the missing pizzelles and the Alzheimer's concern, and now here he was.

"This isn't about me, Anthony. You've got a lot on your hands right now, with your father and Lucy and the divorce—"

"What?" He leaned in, stared at her. "How did you hear about that?"

She leveled her hazel eyes on him and said, "Lucy told us. Actually, she told us quite a bit more than that. She's one confused young woman and she's going to need you by her side until she can straighten things out."

"So I'm supposed to sit by and pretend I'm not upset about this pregnancy?"

"Of course not. But try not to judge." Her voice dipped. "Give her some time and see if she opens up to you."

For a split second, he wished he were dealing with his father's health instead of his daughter's pregnancy. He'd take the old man for testing, meet with doctors, develop a plan, and pick up his medication. That was doable, all within the realm of a son helping his father. Society accepted it, even applauded the child for coordinating the care. But what could he do for his pregnant daughter? Everyone would know. Then what? He knew nothing of pregnancy and baby classes, and could barely remember Lucy being a baby. What was he going to do?

What the hell was he going to do?

"Here. Drink this." Miriam eased a glass filled with two ice cubes and an amber liquid toward him. When had she gotten them drinks? He'd been so preoccupied with his dilemma he hadn't noticed, and he usually noticed everything.

He took a healthy swallow and enjoyed the burn. Bourbon. Two more of these and he might be calm enough to head back into the dining room and face the crowd. Or not.

"I know it doesn't seem like it now," Miriam said, tracing the rim of her glass with an index finger, "but things will work out."

Anthony picked up on the first part of her words and ignored the second. "You're right. It doesn't seem like it."

Before Miriam could respond, the kitchen door opened and Harry Blacksworth appeared carrying a tray of lasagna. "Don't think either of you are leaving without leftovers. We've got enough food to feed half the street for three days."

"That's because we all know how much you love Italian food," Miriam said, humor in her voice. "I'll bet it's gone in two days."

Harry Blacksworth belted out a laugh. "That's the problem. It *will* be gone if I'm left alone with it." He patted his stomach and hefted a sigh. "And that would create ten pounds worth of problems." He glanced at Anthony and said, "There's a half tray of lasagna out there. Pop loves that stuff. How about we wrap it up and send it home with you?"

Anthony wasn't used to people sending him home with doggie bags. Where he lived, the crowd concentrated more on presentation than substance, and the only seconds a person went after were drinks. The offer of food to take home and enjoy later was an unfamiliar gesture, and one that made Anthony uncomfortable. But he didn't want to offend the man or his hospitality, so he nodded and mumbled, "Thank you."

"Welcome."

Miriam finished her drink and stood. "I think I'll head back to the dining room. I wanted to try Greta's antipasto."

"Better hurry, before Pop polishes it all off." Harry Blacksworth slid onto the chair Miriam had just vacated and said, "Says he's developed a new fondness for antipasto prepared German style, whatever that means."

Miriam laughed and shook her head. "With Pop you never know. I'm off to fight him over the last forkful."

When she disappeared into the dining room, Harry Blacksworth reached for the bourbon, unscrewed the top, and poured himself a drink. "Refill?"

Anthony shook his head. He'd already created one scene; he wasn't about to get drunk and create another. "Can I ask you a question?" He might not have another opportunity and who better to ask than the man himself?

"Shoot." Harry Blacksworth sipped his drink and eyed Anthony.

"How did you end up here? It's obvious you're a city guy, so what's your story?"

The man shrugged. "Not much of a story. My niece lives here with her family and my wife and kids fell in love with the town and the people."

There was something in the way he hesitated and those blue eyes looked away for a half second that made Anthony wonder about the rest of the story, the parts where the gaps were. "And you don't miss...Chicago, right?"

"Yup."

"Chicago," he repeated, remembering the times he'd visited, the exhilaration of mixing with the crowds and the energy of the place. "I love Chicago. There's so much happening there, and the people. Sharp dressers." He scanned Harry Blacksworth's burgundy sweater and gray slacks. "And talk about great food. I've never seen so many premiere restaurants in a two-mile radius." Just thinking about the place excited him. He'd loved the feel of the city, had wanted to get back there, maybe take Lucy on a shopping trip. His excitement flopped on his head as he pictured his daughter in a maternity shirt. That hadn't exactly been the type of shopping he'd been thinking about. Anthony ran a hand over his face, pushed thoughts of his daughter's pregnant belly from his brain, and said in a low voice, "You really don't miss it?"

The man opened his mouth to answer, hesitated, and blurted out, "Some days I wonder what the hell I'm doing in a place that doesn't have valet parking or a private country club." His expression softened, matched his words. "And then I look at my wife and kids and I think about the open space, the trees, the grass, the people. It's good for them." He paused. "It's good for me. Keeps me grounded and doesn't let me get too full of myself. It's the little things I look forward to, like the weekly breakfasts with your dad at Lina's Café, the tormenting I get from my niece's husband because the only screwdriver I know is a drink, and spending time with my family."

"Sounds very…suburban." *Who was this guy kidding?* He had to miss the city, especially a place like Chicago. Harry Blacksworth looked like a high-rolling playboy, albeit a reformed one, and that kind never completely settled down.

Harry threw back the rest of his drink, set the glass on the countertop. "You mean boring, right?" He eyed Anthony a second too long, forcing him to look away. "I've heard it all before. You're just putting up a front, you'll show your true colors soon enough, you'll never stay in that town. You know what the odd thing is? I don't hear that from people in this town. No, that sort of trash talk comes from my old golf partners and business associates, the ones living their miserable lives with their wives and mistresses. They're so damn afraid to make a move that might upset their portfolio and standard of living, they'd rather be miserable than take a chance at finding a way to be happy."

"Happy is a relative term." He'd thought he was happy for a lot of years, until he realized he wasn't.

"Right. And unhappy is the result of lying to yourself. At some point, we all have to look in the mirror and it can be an ugly face looking back." He blew out a breath and continued, "That's when choice comes in. Change what you see, or pretend you don't see it." Harry pointed at Anthony and said, "It's the pretending that will take you down faster than a bottle of bourbon, and then you've got nothing, maybe not even your life."

What was he talking about? A piece of Anthony knew exactly what Harry Blacksworth meant because he'd felt this same way once or twice in his life and it had scared the hell out of him. He pushed the feelings away with the same force and denial he had before. "So, I shouldn't pretend to like this town or want to be here a second longer than necessary?" *See what the playboy turned philosopher had to say to that.* What he had to say was…nothing. Anthony cleared his throat, waited for a response that didn't come, and decided on another angle. "Well? No comment?"

Harry shrugged, eyed his empty glass, then shifted his gaze to Anthony. *Damn*, but the knowing look in those eyes said more than a dictionary could. "You sound a lot like I used to back in the day, when I was running after every skirt and running from myself. It's a miserable existence. Here you are with loads of money, suits, cars, vacations, women, all those *things* that you think you need to find real peace and satisfaction. Only, guess what? The more you take, the more you fall into hell until you don't know how to climb out." He poured another drink, refilled Anthony's. "So, you drink more, screw more, lie more…one big, vicious, friggin' cycle. And then something or maybe *someone* comes along and forces you to think about the messed-up existence you call living. For me, it was my niece, and later, my wife. For you, I'm going to say it's your pregnant daughter."

Anthony gulped his drink, coughed, and sputtered. Harry Blacksworth had a lot of practice with his liquor because he'd taken an even bigger drink and acted like it was water. The man laughed, set his glass down, and pointed to it. "Takes practice."

"I am not going to look at my pregnant daughter like she's my salvation. There's not a damn thing wrong with me; it's everybody else, starting with my father's refusal to admit he's old and needs help."

The laugh that followed that statement was belly deep and turned Blacksworth's face redder than the spaghetti sauce they'd eaten earlier. "Your old man is sharper than that whole room out there." He paused, added, "With the exception of Lily, who sees things the rest of us don't."

"Lily? The girl with—"

"Hey, hey, don't you dare label her, or I'm going to have to land my best right hook."

The man was serious. "I didn't mean anything by it. I'm sure she's a nice girl, it's just that..." *Why did he have to explain it? Couldn't Blacksworth see for himself that the girl had Down syndrome?*

"Just what?"

So he wanted him to say it? And then what, land a punch that sent Anthony sprawling? There was more than one way to say something without actually saying it. "She's not like everybody else." *Read between the lines.*

Harry Blacksworth's eyes narrowed, his mouth flattened. "No, she's not. She's a helluva lot better. Lily brings out the best in all of us, makes us see ordinary things in a different way. She makes us want to be better because she thinks we're better than we are." The left side of his jaw twitched and he clenched a fist so hard, Anthony wondered if the man planned to lunge at him. "And there's too many damn fools out there who can't see past a face or a label."

Okay, Anthony did not want to get into a discussion about a child and her abilities or disabilities. He wanted to talk about his father. "I didn't mean to offend anybody; I'm just taking a look from the outside and telling you what I see."

"Right, and I'm telling you what you're seeing isn't there."

Anthony sipped his bourbon, considered his next tactic. "This isn't about Lily Desantro; it's about my father. He thinks he can still live on his own, eat those damnable pizzelles for dinner, take off for walks without anybody knowing—" his breath came in quick forced gasps "—do whatever he wants to do like he's thirty-five, not seventy-five."

"And that's a problem? Other than the pizzelles for dinner…"

"Hell, yes, it's a problem. He's seventy-five!"

Harry Blacksworth shook his head. "Tony, Tony, why so rigid? Pop might have been walking this earth for over seventy years, but he's younger in heart and spirit than either of us."

That was not the point. "He's going to start failing and who's going to help him? What if he falls again? Or really does get confused? Someone needs to keep an eye on him. And do you know he talks to my mother every day? She died almost three years ago."

"Pop says your mother lives in his heart. Can't argue with a man who tells you that."

"But he *talks* to her like she's sitting next to him."

"Yup. Ever try it?" Harry Blacksworth cocked his head to the side, studied Anthony a second too long. "You should. Very peaceful, kind of gives you that 'other world' feel."

"This whole town is nuts," Anthony muttered. "I can't wait to get out of here."

"You might be waiting a little longer than planned." He crossed his arms over his chest and pinned him with a blue-eyed stare. "There's a storm coming and it's a big one."

Chapter 5

Snow and wind swept over the mountains into Magdalena, blanketing the hills in white, creating three-foot drifts that made it difficult to navigate roads leading in or out of town without a four-wheel drive. Even then, if a person were unfamiliar with the area, he'd do better to stay home and stay warm lest he risk ending up in a ditch on the side of the road.

Nate had grown up in this town and had barreled his way down more than one snow-packed road. If he waited for the snow to melt or settle, he might be waiting until spring, and he was not a patient man. He was, however, a man who trusted his own abilities, and driving in inclement conditions such as snow was an area where he excelled. This was why he'd been delegated to pick up Ben and Gina Reed and drive them to Cash and Tess's with Christine, where they'd enjoy a batch of Cash's signature chili along with Jeremy Dean's homemade sourdough bread and finish up with Nate's double fudge brownies. Of course, this was supposed to be a working dinner, as in planning the upcoming Christmas gift deliveries to the needy on behalf of The Bleeding Hearts Society and an anonymous donor, who they all guessed was Harry Blacksworth. When Nate learned of the very generous gift donations ranging from electronics to clothes, to toys, bedding, bicycles, housewares, even pet supplies, he pegged the donor as Harry.

People confronted Harry, some in a bold manner, others with sly comments and insinuations, but no matter the person, the method, or the number of inquiries, they got nothing from Harry Blacksworth other than a shrug and an

"I don't know what the hell you're talking about."

Nate, Cash, and Ben planned to deliver the gifts to the names on Mimi Pendergrass's list, beginning three days before Christmas. The Bleeding Hearts Society had begun the wrapping process, but there were so many extra gifts with the anonymous giver's donation that Christine, Tess, and Gina decided to help out and organize their own wrapping party at Tess's house. And that's where they were now, eating chili, sampling Jeremy Dean's sourdough bread, and already thinking about Nate's double fudge brownies.

"So, what's the deal on Pop's son?" Cash tore off a hunk of bread and dipped it in his chili. "He sounds like a jerk."

"Or a real city boy," Ben said, sliding a glance at Nate. "You know the kind: pain in the ass, know-it-all, arrogant."

Nate eyed him from across the table, lifted his beer bottle, and took a swig. "Yeah, he's got a name, too." He paused, his lips working into a faint smile. "Ben Reed."

Cash slapped his knee and laughed. "Oh, that's classic."

Gina smiled at her husband, who pretended irritation. "He does have a point, Ben." She gentled her voice in a way Nate wouldn't have thought possible six months ago. "You did have a bit of an air about you."

"Yeah, hot air," Cash added, breaking into another round of laughter.

Tess and Christine hid their smiles and Nate shook his head. Who would have thought he'd end up actually liking Ben Reed enough to call him a friend? Not Nate, that was for damn sure, but once the guy admitted he loved Gina, everything changed. He became a real human being with a sense of humor, and Nate wouldn't forget how he helped Jeremy Ross Dean get out of police work or the way he confided in Mimi Pendergrass like she was a relative. Mimi needed that, and Ben had needed it, too. Christine said one of the biggest miracles was the transformation of Gina Servetti into Gina Reed, a woman of confidence, beauty, compassion, and the ability to forgive her parents for doing her wrong. That didn't mean she invited them for Sunday dinner, but the forgiveness part was a start. Nate heard all of this from Christine, who heard bits and pieces of it from Gina, Tess, even Bree, though Bree Kinkaid hadn't been around much because she'd been too busy learning her father's business. That was another story and another hornet's nest just waiting for a swat.

The man spreading the information like fertilizer on his tomato plants was Pop Benito, Godfather and Matchmaker of Magdalena as well as Grand Gossiper of the town. He knew more than anybody and what he didn't know, he surmised, or made up his mind to find out. But now Pop was the one who needed help and it was up to the town to see he got it.

Even if it meant finding a way to boot his only son out of town.

"I think Anthony's in a difficult situation." Christine glanced around the table and shrugged. "Coming here and knowing nothing about Lucy. I can't imagine the shock."

"And then demanding Pop and Lucy go back to California with him." Gina shook her head and sighed. "I'll bet that conversation went from bad to worse before he finished his sentence."

"If the guy cares so much, why is this the first time he's been back—" Cash paused, rubbed his jaw "—in how long?"

"A long time," Nate said. He was the only one who really knew the timeline of Anthony Benito's coming and goings to and from Magdalena. Christine and Ben weren't from here, Gina had been at school, and Tess and Cash…well, they'd suffered their own brand of misery that took them from town.

"I feel kind of sorry for him," Tess said, her voice soft, low. "He's obviously unhappy and his family situation is messed up with a divorce and a pregnant daughter, but that doesn't mean he doesn't care and isn't worried about Lucy and Pop."

"Maybe." Cash slathered butter onto a piece of Jeremy Dean's sourdough bread and said, "But that doesn't mean he has the right to make demands. It's like charging into battle when you don't know where the battle is or who's on your side."

"So what's the plan?" Ben asked. "Or should I say, *is* there a plan?"

"I think that depends on Pop and Lucy." Christine cleared her throat and said, "If Pop wants to stay, there are enough of us in this town to keep an eye on him. Uncle Harry has even volunteered to check on him every day." She paused, added, "*If* he needs help."

"And we've got Lucy covered, too," Tess said. "I'll take her to her doctor visits and maybe when the time comes, even be her coach in the labor room."

"Tess." Cash clasped her hand, his expression fierce. "I don't think the labor room is a good idea."

"Why not?" she asked in a too-bright voice. "She's going to need someone."

He shook his head, touched her cheek. "We'll talk about it, okay?"

Nate looked away, not wanting to witness the sadness on their faces: Tess because she couldn't get pregnant, and Cash because he couldn't protect her from that pain. They were good people, they'd make great parents, and yet they hadn't been able to get pregnant. How long did they wait before they tried adoption or fostering? It wasn't a conversation men had with their buddies. That's what women did: talked about temperature charts and periods and pregnancies. Why did Tess torment herself by volunteering to take Lucy for her prenatal visits? And the part about becoming a labor room coach? What the hell had prompted that? It would be disastrous on so many levels; Cash must have seen it and that's why he'd intervened. What a damn sad place this world could be.

Christine touched his shirtsleeve and when he met her gaze, she moved her head the slightest bit. He knew what that meant. They'd talked about telling everyone the news tonight, but Nate didn't need a degree in psychology or his wife's head shake to know this wasn't the time to add one more pregnancy revelation to Cash and Tess's sadness. There would be time enough when things settled down with Pop and Lucy. He squeezed his wife's hand, let her know he understood. Somewhere between the first time he saw Christine, when his heart had been so filled with hatred and resentment, to now, when they were pregnant with their second child, he'd become more human and aware of other people's feelings. That's what loving Christine had done for him and he thanked God for that.

***

Ramona Casherdon was on a mission and in order to accomplish it, she had to get Lucy Benito out of earshot and eyeball range of Miriam Desantro. What Ramona had to say was private and required a one-on-one conversation with no outside interruptions. That would never happen if Miriam Desantro were on the other side of Harry Blacksworth's kitchen counter, dissecting gestures, tone of voice, and other nuances that might help her interpret the conversation. Ramona couldn't label her a nosy woman because she wasn't. Strong-minded? Champion of the underdog? Willing to take up a fight for what she believed was right? Yes to all of the aforementioned, and Ramona could not afford an intrusion when she had important matters to discuss with Lucy Benito, so important as to offer the girl a private pumpkin roll making lesson at her house.

She didn't invite people to her home with the exception of Cash, and now, Tess, but they were family. And if she stretched the "family line" a bit, she supposed she could include Tess's mother, Olivia, and her husband, Will Carrick. They'd been Ramona's friends before they became "family" though JJ Carrick's death had caused a falling out between Ramona and Olivia for too many years. But now they were on an even keel again, and while neither woman blabbered on and on about the lost years of friendship, they did on occasion enjoy a cup of coffee together and a baking session. There was always a new recipe to try and an opinion to be gained on the flakiness of the pie crust, the creaminess of the frosting, the richness of the custard.

Ramona glanced around the tiny kitchen, took in the aging appliances, the discolored and worn Formica countertop, the dull stainless steel sink. There were stacks of cookbooks, coffee cups, and potholders on the counters; a bowl of plastic Granny Smith apples, a bowl of *real* McIntosh apples, and her one concession to pampered luxury—a coffee maker with a built-in grinder and specialty blends that performed all manner of magic; they woke her up, relaxed her, and, shock upon shock, they made her smile. The coffee maker was a gift from Cash and Tess, who, upon witnessing the not-often-seen smile on

Ramona's face, elected an automatic refill option that delivered a specialty blend to her doorstep once a month.

If Ramona were alone, she'd choose an aromatic decaffeinated coffee, the kind she and Olivia enjoyed for their after-6:00 p.m. visits. But with a pregnant girl, green tea seemed the more appropriate choice. Ramona set out the tea, put the pot on low, and waited.

The girl arrived a short time later, her pale face red and wet from the cold and snow, her blue eyes a mirror of her grandmother's. She had her grandmother's red hair, too, and her nose. "I really appreciate this, Mrs. Casherdon. My grandpa's going to be so surprised when I bring him a pumpkin roll." She shrugged out of her jacket and smoothed her sweatshirt over her belly. "I'll bet he tries to dig into it tonight." She laughed and pulled off her boots to reveal small feet covered in red and green candy cane socks.

She's just a child, a baby having a baby.

Ramona nodded, forced a tight smile, and said, "The name's Ramona." She didn't correct her on the misuse of Mrs. What was the point? Everyone but Lucy Benito knew Ramona didn't have a husband; as far as they knew, she'd never had a husband, never even had a boyfriend. That would not be exactly correct, but what she did or did not have, including surnames, was not their business.

"Oh." The girl's face turned redder. "Sure. Sorry," she mumbled, and then finished with, "Ramona."

It would not do to have the girl nervous before Ramona had a chance to execute her plan. But first, they had baking to do and tea to drink. "I've set out the ingredients. Dry over here—" she pointed to the flour, baking powder, cinnamon. and other spices "—and wet such as oil, pumpkin, eggs, and vanilla, over here. If you follow the recipe, you'll know exactly how to combine the ingredients and that's important. Too many beginners toss everything in all at once and then wonder why their cake is flat and doesn't rise. There's an art to it."

"Like Grandpa's pizzelles," Lucy Benito said, studying the recipe. "He says people are in too much of a rush and that's why they mess up. They haven't finished the first task and they're already on the third."

"Your grandfather is a wise man."

The girl smiled and her voice softened. "He's the wisest man I know."

Ramona spent the next hour teaching the girl how to measure properly, what happens when you overbeat the mixture, why you should always crack eggs in a separate bowl, and how to check for doneness that had nothing to do with a timer. With Ramona's supervision, Lucy Benito poured the batter into the prepared baking pan, placed it in the oven, and went to work on the cream cheese filling. "Most people can't afford pecans, so walnuts are a cheaper choice." Ramona opened the first package of cream cheese and set it aside. "Not that walnuts are cheap, but every penny saved helps, and—" She caught herself before she went on about the importance of being thrifty. What would this child know about cutting costs, buying seconds, or going without?

"Grandpa says we shouldn't be wasteful, that one pair of shoes might not be enough but four is too much." The girl measured the walnuts and dumped them in a small chopper. "He said Grandma washed out her plastic bags and reused the broccoli rubber bands." She laughed and glanced at Ramona. "My grandma was a recycler before it was cool to recycle."

Ramona shrugged, uncomfortable with the warmth in

the girl's eyes. "That's called being practical. If more people in this world thought like her, they'd have more money and fewer garbage problems."

"That's what Grandpa says. I tried to recycle, but Dad kept getting mixed up between recyclable and non-recyclable, so I gave up."

"You can't give up when something gets hard." Ramona dumped the second cream cheese in the mixing bowl and stirred. "That's when real character comes out. Weak people give up at the first obstacle, but the strong ones, they grow more determined, and they keep going."

"Is that what happened with your nephew, Cash?"

Ramona shot her a look, clenched the spatula in her right hand. She did not like anyone talking about her nephew and if they did, she wanted to know what they were saying. "Who told you that?"

The girl paled. "Grandpa told me about his injury," she stammered.

Fine, the injury was something Ramona could handle. It was the other…

"And that he and Tess…"

"He and Tess, what?" *Damn that Pop for opening his mouth.*

"…were torn apart before the marriage."

Ramona let out a sigh. That she could handle, too. The whole town knew of the tragic events that separated Cash and Tess, and they'd also witnessed the reunion that led them down the aisle. Maybe Pop was trying to show his granddaughter a silver lining in their story and, in that way, help her find one in her own predicament.

"I really like Tess. She's been so kind." She placed a hand on her belly and said, "She takes me to my doctor visits and even offered to be my coach when the time comes."

"Your coach?" How had Ramona not known about Tess taking Lucy Benito to her prenatal visits? That was a bad idea on so many levels. Why hadn't Cash stepped in and said something? Or maybe he had and it hadn't worked.

"Uh-huh. But I don't know. I feel kind of bad, you know...with Tess and Cash not being able to have their own baby and all."

"Who told you *that?*" If it had been Pop, she'd give him a piece of her mind, and it wouldn't be good.

The girl blinked hard. "I'm sorry. I didn't mean to upset you."

"Who told you?"

"Tess."

Ramona could not have heard that right. "Tess?"

"She told me how she almost got rid of the baby but changed her mind...and then she lost it...and there was an infection and scarring..." A tear slipped down her cheek, then another, and she swiped at them with both hands. "She said she never told Cash until years later, after they got back together, and only because he found out. At first he was so angry, but he forgave her and said if they couldn't have children of their own, they'd adopt or whatever, as long as they were together." She sniffed, sniffed again. "She said I wasn't alone; the whole town cared about me and no matter what, people were there for me. Imagine her telling me that when I'm pregnant with a baby I didn't even want and she can't get pregnant. How absolutely tragic is that?"

More tears poured out as the girl's slender body shook and she whimpered her grief. Ramona stood there, one hand gripping the countertop, the other clutching the spatula, torn between comforting Lucy Benito and using this time as an opportunity to accomplish her mission. She released the spatula and placed a hand on the girl's shoulder. "Maybe you can find it in your heart to help Tess and Cash get through their pain."

Lucy Benito swiped her hands across her face and nodded. "What can I do?"

Ramona leaned toward her, placed a hand on the girl's swollen belly, and said, "Give them your child."

Chapter 6

Anthony hadn't driven in this much snow in over twenty-five years, but that didn't stop him from yanking on his coat and grabbing the car keys two seconds after Lucy told him and Pop that Ramona Casherdon had asked her to give up her baby to Cash and Tess Casherdron. *Who the hell did that woman think she was?* A person didn't go around making those kinds of requests, especially to a vulnerable, pregnant young girl, one who happened to be his daughter. He should have paid closer attention to the dynamics going on around him. He had no idea Ramona's nephew and his wife couldn't have a child, or that Ramona had invited Lucy to her home supposedly to teach her to make a pumpkin roll. That woman hadn't changed; all these years later she was still doing whatever she wanted and to hell with everybody else.

Not this time. Anthony was going to call her on her reckless behavior and then he was going to demand she apologize to his daughter. Nobody had a right to treat Lucy that way. He made it to Ramona Casherdon's tiny house with only one skid and remembering to pump the brakes well before the stop signs.

Damn you, Ramona! He slammed the door, trudged up the unshoveled driveway, and made his way to her front porch. Only a glimmer of light shone through the drawn curtains. She'd always been partial to night and darkness, and there'd been a time when he was, too. Despite the lack of activity or illumination, Ramona Casherdon was in that house; he was certain of it. He rang the doorbell and waited, angry with himself for not thinking this through but angrier with her for putting him in this position.

The door eased open and there she stood, a figure cast in shadows by the faint light behind her. He couldn't make out her features or the expression on her face, and until she spoke in that husky voice he'd never been able to forget, the woman could have been anybody. "Hello, Tony. I've been expecting you." Once she said his name, it all came back, the memories, the pain, the longing, in sharp, lasting, and dreaded detail.

"Hello, Ramona." He forced the emotion from his voice as he faced the woman who'd cast him aside so many years ago. "May I come in?" The shadowed figure opened the door wider, stepped aside. Ramona had never been one for talking much, preferred to show her feelings through actions. Anthony had been the one to go on and on like a sick poet, until she laughed and demanded he stop expounding on her "supposed" beauty and virtues. He hadn't wanted to, though; he'd been so enraptured with the essence and mystique of Ramona Casherdon that he never wanted to stop talking to her or about her.

Unfortunately, she'd found a way to shut off the spouting—permanently.

She turned away and began gathering a stack of magazines from the couch as though she were in no particular hurry to face him, as though she'd seen him yesterday instead of twenty-eight years ago. She was broader than he remembered, shorter, too, dressed in black pants and a black top, her long black hair streaked with gray and pulled into a loose bun. The large gold hoops she favored dangled from her ears. He'd wanted to buy her diamond studs, or rubies, but she'd refused, just as she'd refused everything else he'd offered, even his love. When she turned, her dark gaze met his and he didn't see that time had rounded her middle, given her extra rolls where there'd been none, and drawn fine wrinkles near her mouth and eyes. Anthony saw *her* as she fit into his memories: the woman who had stolen his heart and cast him aside.

"You're here about your daughter."

How could she look at him with such casualness as though seeing him or not seeing him was of no consequence? Her nonchalance annoyed him and it spilled over into his next words. "My daughter is not going to hand over her baby to your nephew and his wife."

Her voice dipped, turned huskier. "And you came to stop me?"

He took a step closer. "Yes."

That seemed to amuse her. "Because you've been able to control what I've done in the past?" She cocked a brow, her full lips hinting at a smile.

"Right," he bit out. "Maybe I've learned a few things since then."

She eyed him as though to say she seriously doubted it and shrugged. "I have no intention of trying to convince your daughter to do anything. I merely said that because I wanted to talk to you and thought that might be the only way to get you here."

Now he was annoyed *and* angry. "You played me? You made Lucy half-hysterical as a ploy to get me here?" How dare she do that? "You couldn't pick up the phone like a normal person and call me?"

"Tony, don't be so dramatic." Those eyes moved over him, pierced him with their intensity. People said she looked like a gypsy and it was more than the dark eyeliner she favored, or the large hoop earrings and bracelets she wore. It wasn't even her penchant for black that had them whispering that word. No, it had to do with the aura she created when she walked into a room, or stood next to someone. She had the ability to draw them in without a word, pull energy from them to interpret their mood, their emotion, their troubles. People stayed away from her, uncomfortable by her silence and intense gaze. Not Anthony. He'd been drawn to her the second he spotted her in Victor's Pharmacy where he'd stopped to pick up a box of candy for his mother. Ramona had been filling a prescription for Cash's sore throat.

"Dramatic? That's my daughter we're talking about, Ramona." He sighed, raked a hand through his hair. She'd always had the ability to unsettle him with a few words.

"And your daughter's the reason I wanted to see you." She gestured to the worn couch and said, "Sit. I'll get you a glass of wine."

He should remain standing but then she'd tack *petty* to *dramatic* so he took a seat on the couch that, upon closer inspection, appeared to be a slightly updated version of the one she'd had twenty-eight years ago. Plaid. Ugly. Cheap. He hadn't cared, hadn't thought about the sound of the loose springs moving with the rhythm of their lovemaking, or the fried oil smell permeating the house. Anthony hadn't noticed any of it because he'd been immersed in Ramona Casherdon.

"Here." She handed him a glass. "Still drink Cabernet?"

He nodded and took a sip. Ramona might call it Cabernet but it burned his throat and tasted more like vinegar. "So, you wanted to talk to me?" It was difficult to pretend nonchalance when he'd spent years imagining this moment, the look on her face when she saw that he'd survived her refusal, and not only that, he'd *thrived*. Except, sitting in this dingy living room in this godforsaken town thousands of miles from California, he didn't feel victorious. Yes, he had money, an important job, and friends who owned season tickets to every sporting and musical event within a fifty-mile radius, but so what? Did it compensate for the mess that had become his world? The life he'd planned did not include an ex-wife, a pregnant and unmarried daughter, or a father who acted as if he were thirty-five. And yet, here he was, sharing a glass of cheap wine with an ex-lover and feeling as worn and beat up as the couch he sat on.

She must have sensed his mood because she sat on the other end of the couch and said in a quiet, yet firm voice, "Your daughter needs you."

"Hmm. You mean to get her out of this mess she's in? Or to talk some sense into her about staying here with my father?"

Ramona's earrings jangled when she shook her head. "I meant she needs you to salvage this relationship. She's scared and hurting and this isn't the time to point fingers and find fault."

"No, that would have been before she got pregnant."

"Tony, if you can't accept this, it's not going to end well."

"Why am I always the one who has to accept things?" He turned toward her, anger simmering beneath his words. "Accept that my daughter's pregnant and doesn't want to talk about it, and refuses to mention the father? Accept that she's determined to quit college and stay in Magdalena? And I even have to accept my father's supposed right to be independent when he isn't? I'm tired of it, tired of not having a say in what other people are doing that affects me."

"Are we talking about them—" she paused, met his gaze "—or are we talking about us?"

And there it was, the real reason behind his agitation

tonight. "Did you ever once regret your decision?"

Her eyes sparked with what might have been annoyance or pain; he couldn't tell. That was the problem with Ramona Casherdon; he'd never been able to tell what she was really thinking or feeling. It was all a mystery and a guessing game. "I don't believe in looking back and wallowing in regret."

That wasn't an answer. "Humor me, Ramona. I would have done anything for you; helped raise Cash, even stayed in Magdalena if that's what you wanted. But you rejected me, and I've always wondered if maybe for a second you ever wished you'd made a different choice."

She looked away. "You were twenty-five, a boy."

Still not an answer. "You were thirty-one. So what?"

"You had your whole life before you, a chance to do big things, no ties. Nothing to hold you back from letting the world sink into your pores. I had responsibilities."

"Cash might have welcomed a male figure in his life instead of an overprotective aunt."

Her gaze sliced over him, glittered in anger. "I gave him love and consistency."

"And two people couldn't have done that?"

She swiped a strand of hair from her face in what looked like an agitated response to his question. "We barely knew each other. I couldn't risk exposing Cash to a relationship that might not work out." She paused, smoothed a wrinkle from her slacks. "Then what? Move the boy back here and pretend we never happened?"

"Isn't that pretty much what you did?" he asked. "You know, the pretending-we-never-happened part?" Oh, she didn't like that comment. Too damn bad. There'd been a lot of things he hadn't liked, starting with refusing to discuss their relationship, but she'd done them anyway.

"I sent you away because I was not going to be responsible for holding you back. You had such dreams and they weren't about making barrels of money." Her voice dipped. "They were about making a difference."

That was before he'd tasted the sweetness of money dipped in expense accounts and year-end bonuses from the advertising company, making anything less seem bitter and inedible. Why would he spend hours teaching high school kids to dissect a sentence and look for symbolism in *Animal Farm* when he could enjoy five-star dinners, sporting events, and fly to New York City, all in the name of business, *and* all on his business account? His mother said he possessed the "gift of gab" and while many struggled with simple conversation, this was an area where he excelled. *Talk, talk, talk, posture, convince, win.* It became a game as he worked to convince naysayers to try a particular product. They argued, he cajoled, they postured, he retreated and let them think they were in charge. Of course, they weren't, and by the next conversation, he'd won them over. It was all a game that paid big money and came too easily for him, until one day last year, it wasn't fun any longer. That's when he knew he was trapped.

"What happened to those dreams, Anthony? Did you sell out?"

The accusation in her question angered him. She had no right to judge him because he'd wanted a better life than his parents. So what? He'd earned everything he had, no handouts or special favors. He finished his wine, set the glass on the coffee table, and said, "I found something I was great at and it made a helluva lot more money than teaching sophomore English."

"And what is that?"

"I convince people to want things they didn't know they

wanted."

"Ah." She tapped a long finger against her chin and nodded. "You take their money."

"No. Why would you say that?"

"You fill their brain with fancy words and make them believe they need things and then you take their money. Money some can't afford to spend."

"That's not true. You don't even know me."

"No. I don't." And then, "Did you do that with me, Tony? Try to make me want something I didn't know I wanted?"

"What?" The cold look on her face spoke of disgust. "Of course not. You're the one who sent me away, remember? And for what? So you could raise your nephew, living in this dump? Do you know what I could have given you, given you both? Do you have any idea?"

"I raised my nephew," she said quietly. "It's a bigger task than you think. No amount of money can pay for the joy of seeing him married and happy."

"So you were an example of married and happy? Somehow I doubt that." That was cruel and unnecessary, but damn it, she'd ripped his heart in two all those years ago. She deserved to feel some pain, too.

Those dark eyes turned black. "Was I happy? Much of the time, I wasn't. Do you know what it's like to have to clean other people's toilets to put food on the table? Or cook fancy meals when you can't afford a cheap cut of meat? Do you have any idea? But I had my pride and my self-respect. No man kept me and no man took advantage of me."

"Good for you. I hope it kept you warm at night."

She squared her shoulders, her expression blank when she said, "You're going to lose your daughter if you don't make amends. The reason she doesn't want to return to California with you is because she doesn't consider it a home, not *her* home." She paused, drew in a deep breath. "Apparently the servants taught her more about family than you and her mother did."

"What?" He stood and paced the small living room. "She didn't say that."

"Oh, but she did, and much more. Seems you and her mother were so busy fattening your bank accounts that you forgot to be parents." She tilted her head in challenge. "I might not be able to build equity, but I do know how to build a relationship with my nephew."

Why would Lucy say that? He could see where Rosalyn might fit into the "un-parent" category, but not him. He loved Lucy. She knew that. Didn't she? *Well, didn't she?*

"If you care about your daughter, you'll listen to her, really listen. The same with your father. He wants to die here, Tony. I know it would be a lot easier if you could pack him up and take him with you like a suitcase, but he's not going. Maybe he and Lucy can watch out for each other."

And what about me? Who am I going to take care of, and who's going to take care of me? He really was all alone, and the pain of knowing that burst through him, burning a path to his heart.

"Tony?" Ramona stood an arm's length away, her lilac scent drifting to him. "I did have regrets once." She met his gaze, held it. "You'd been gone three months. I couldn't sleep, couldn't get through the day without wondering how life might have been had I said 'yes' to you. The wondering lived in my soul, threatened to suffocate me, until one day I decided to call."

"No." He shook his head. "I never got a call from you."

"A man answered the phone and when I asked for you, he told me you were at an engagement party." She paused, her eyes so bright he had to look away. "Yours."

***

Christmas was coming to Magdalena in less than seventy-two hours and this year, like so many others, there would indeed be a white Christmas. The snow had tapered to flurries last night, a welcome relief among the adults, while the children hoped for even more of the white stuff—the better to build forts, snowmen, snowladies, even snow dogs!

Nate, Cash, and Ben loaded up the SUV to deliver the third round of gifts on The Bleeding Hearts Society Christmas list. They'd started the deliveries this morning, heading to the outskirts of town first and working their way toward Main Street using the spreadsheets Christine and Gina had created. Nate knew his wife specialized in organization, but with Gina at her side, it was a little too organized. Color coding? Pie charts according to area? Was it really necessary? What would they say if they knew there'd been no spreadsheet in the past, no charts either, pie or otherwise, and they hadn't missed a single home? Nate didn't think he'd mention that because Christine and Gina were so darned proud of those sheets.

"You know we're supposed to get dumped on tonight, right?" Cash peered out the front window of the SUV. "Damn, but it's going to get interesting."

Ben sighed from the back seat where he sat wedged in by the overflow of gifts. "Yeah, looks like I'll be trading in the car for a four-wheel drive."

Cash laughed. "Welcome to the husbands' club, right, Nate?"

Nate smiled. "You're going to have bigger headaches

when Gina puts a For Sale sign on that Harley."

"Huh? That is not happening." When Nate shrugged, Ben went on. "You think she'll want me to get rid of it?" There was some serious worry in his voice. "I love that bike. I can't get rid of it." Big sigh. "Damn." And then, "I'm going to have to get rid of that bike."

"Hey, Nate's just ragging on you." Cash grinned and shook his head. "He still likes to see you squirm."

"Who, me?" Nate shot Cash a look. "Would I do that to the police sergeant of Magdalena?"

Another laugh from Cash. "Hell yes, you would."

"You're right." Nate's smile spread. "Relax, Ben. Gina might have forgotten it's sitting in Philly waiting for you." He paused, added, "Then again, that wife of yours doesn't forget a thing. Unless the pregnancy hormones take over and she's too preoccupied with the baby to think about your toys."

"Well, don't say anything," Ben said. "I want to work it into the conversation, not just spring it on her."

"Don't wait too long," Nate said, glancing in the rearview mirror. "Gina won't like that."

"Yeah, women don't like surprises that have to do with your past." Cash blew out a long breath and muttered, "Especially if they weren't part of it."

He was talking about Ben's cousin, Paige Reed, and the visit she paid to Magdalena that almost destroyed the fragile bond between Cash and Tess. Nate knew about pasts and people who wanted to dredge them up and create all kinds of turmoil and insecurities. Hadn't Gloria Blacksworth tried her damnedest to use Natalie Servetti to break up his marriage? Who knew what other evil she'd have orchestrated if she'd lived longer? Thoughts of his mother-in-law made him remember the notebook in his desk drawer at work. He'd have to do something about it soon. Part of him wanted to open it and see what vile Gloria had conjured up, but he hesitated. Once he read the words he wouldn't be able to forget them, even if they weren't true. And that's where the other part came in, the one that wanted to throw the sucker in the fire and watch it burn. He would have done it by now if not for Christine. She hadn't mentioned the damn thing in months, but that didn't mean she'd forgotten about it and he wasn't going to ask her, so he'd stay in limbo, waiting...for now.

"So what's the story on this Androvich guy who's coming to visit Bree's father's place?" Ben asked. "Bree seems pretty upset about it."

"Androvich?" Cash asked. "Never heard of him."

Nate shrugged. "Me either. Who is he?"

"I guess he's part owner of the lumber company that provides black cherry to Bree's dad. The guy's in Pennsylvania; Bree said their fathers were friends back in the day."

"Hmm." Cash rubbed his jaw, sliced a look at Ben. "Maybe he heard there's going to be a Harley for sale in Philly and wants to talk to the owner personally."

"Asshole," Ben muttered.

Cash grinned and then turned serious. "Bree's pretty jumpy right now, especially with that jerk husband always on her about working at her dad's place. Androvich might just want to do a little PR and try to sell more lumber, who knows?"

"Bree's worried her dad will want to bring in this Androvich to run the place and she'll lose her chance," Ben said.

"When's the guy coming?" Nate asked.

"No idea." This from Ben.

"I'll talk to Rex and see what I can find out. Tell Bree to try and relax; she's got enough problems right now without looking for more." Nate was so busy thinking about Bree and Brody Kinkaid and their mounting issues that he almost missed the first delivery address.

"Hey, Nate, there's our stop." Cash pointed to the brown ranch where Joy Hammond lived with her two young children and her wheelchair-bound mother. Nate pulled into the driveway, while Ben grabbed the bag of gifts marked for the Hammonds and opened the door.

"Be right back." He hopped out of the SUV and headed up the driveway.

"Who would have thought...?" Cash said, watching Ben greet Joy Hammond with a big smile and the bag of gifts.

"Not me," Nate muttered. "Never saw him as a domesticated prospect, especially not here."

"Especially not domesticated by Gina," Cash added.

Ben waved good-bye to Joy and made his way toward the SUV, whistling.

"Yeah, goes to show, you just never know." Cash laughed. "Even when you think you do."

Chapter 7

Harry Blacksworth didn't do anything small-scale, especially on Christmas Eve. Charlie used to say that if Harry could throw a party on the moon, he would. Oh, but she wished Charlie could see Harry now: married, a father and stepfather. Content with life, happy. The town loved his loud laughs, wide smiles, and silly jokes. Word had it he often paid for random customers at Lina's Café and escaped before anyone knew the mystery benefactor. Word got out, though, and with it, a greater respect and appreciation for the Chicago playboy-turned-husband and small-town resident. Nothing created a bigger "splash" than the darn pool he built. People hoped for an invitation and if they didn't receive one, figured out how to get one, usually by way of Greta. Harry Blacksworth would do anything for his wife, and it did a heart good to see that kind of love.

Miriam sucked in a deep breath, placed a hand on her chest to ease the ache. *I miss you, Charlie. Every day and every night. This pain is never going to go away, not until I close my eyes for the last time. But it's worth it, all of it. I love you, Charlie Blacksworth; I'll always love you.* She sniffed, cleared her throat. *If you could see your little brother right now, you'd be so proud of him. He's grown up, he really has. Merry Christmas, my love. Until we meet again, you hold my heart.*

"Mom, look at this place! It's all sparkly." Lily dropped the shopping bags filled with presents and made a slow circle, eyeing the snow-covered garland, the life-sized toy soldiers, the silver and gold wreaths. "Beautiful," she whispered. When she caught sight of a three-foot twinkling angel suspended from the ceiling, she ran to it. "Wow! An angel!" She scrunched her nose and glanced at the glittery lettering on the angel's wings. "L-I-L-Y," she read. "Lily. Lily! That's me!" Her blue eyes sparkled brighter than the suspended angel. "That's me, Mom!"

Miriam nodded and pointed to another angel in the corner of the room. "How about that one?"

Lily ran to the second angel, read the glittery name on it. "Lizzie." She laughed. "Lizzie's an angel, too." She looked at Miriam, excitement and wonder splashing across her face. "Is there one for Jackson and AJ, too? And Anna?"

"I don't know, but I think you should check, don't you?"

Lily nodded and said, "Uh-huh." And then, "I'm an angel." She twirled around once, twice, almost lost her balance. "I'm an angel, Mom."

Miriam blinked hard, smiled at her daughter, and said, "Yes, dear, you're an angel."

"After I find the angels, I'm going to find Uncle Harry." She paused, glanced at the large Christmas tree in the living room. "He said I could help put presents under the tree. They have five trees. Do you think we're going to put presents under all of them?"

"With your uncle in charge, I have no idea."

Lily giggled. "Uncle Harry always has a good plan. He's probably wrapping presents right now."

Miriam stifled a laugh. "Oh, I doubt that."

"Why? Do you think he doesn't know how?"

This time Miriam did laugh. "I'm sure he doesn't know how, Lily, but if you find him, tell him he needs to get wrapping. You may have to teach him."

A smile burst across Lily's face. "I'm a good wrapper. See you later, Mom." She headed toward the winding staircase, her ponytail bouncing back and forth against the back of her lavender velour outfit.

Miriam shook her head and made her way to the room that often provided the most comfort: the kitchen. She did not expect to find Ramona Casherdon there, spooning sauce over a tray of manicotti. "Ramona? What are you doing here?" Everyone knew the woman didn't socialize, limited her interactions to her nephew and his wife and the people who paid her to clean their houses and cook their meals. Engaging in conversation and spending time with people for the pure enjoyment of it? Well, that would not be something anyone in this town would link to Ramona Casherdon.

"Surprise." She eyed Miriam with what might be close to a half smile. "Harry asked me to help out." She paused and stumbled over her next words, "And stay for dinner."

"Oh." Their gazes locked, Ramona daring Miriam to comment on what they both knew was an odd situation. "Well then. Let me find an apron and tell me what I can do to help."

For the next hour, they worked side by side, making up trays of manicotti, arranging meat and cheese platters, slicing pumpkin rolls, and organizing the Blacksworth Christmas Eve dinner. They didn't talk much, but after an initial awkwardness, Miriam actually enjoyed working with Ramona. Her skilled hands and cooking knowledge made preparing food for such a large event so much easier. When they did speak, it was Ramona who began the conversation and in typical fashion, she got right to her point.

"Ever wonder why women like us end up alone?"

Miriam was slicing a cucumber for the salad, and that comment stopped her. "What?"

Ramona slid her a look, those dark eyes almost black. "Women like us. Are we too independent? Too picky?" She tilted her head and the gold earrings she always wore jangled against her neck. "Or do we know there'll never be another one like the one we lost, so we shut down that part of our life? What do you think?"

What Miriam thought was that she'd like to know who Ramona had loved and lost. It had to have been someone from before she landed in Magdalena because no one had ever seen her with a man, though in the beginning, several had tried to elicit her interest. With no success.

"Well?"

The woman really expected an answer. Okay, she'd give her one. "All of the above."

"What?"

Miriam shrugged and tossed several slices of cucumber in the salad bowl. "I'd rather be alone than with someone for the pure sake of avoiding loneliness, because it backfires and then you're really miserable. I've lived that life and I swore I'd never do it again." She paused and her voice shifted to the softness of remembering. "I wasn't looking for a man when Charlie came along, but there he was, at Sal's Market in the pickle aisle, searching for kosher dills. I needed chocolate chips for the cookies I promised Jack Finnegan." She glanced at Ramona, held her gaze. "If Jack hadn't asked for those cookies, I might never have met Charlie."

"I'd say destiny had something to say about that."

"Yes, I believe that's true." She would not have thought Ramona Casherdon believed in destiny, but apparently the woman did. Maybe they had more in common than Miriam thought. "Charlie was the kindest, gentlest, most tormented soul I'd ever met. He was grieving the loss of his younger sister who'd died from cancer and questioning so many things: his life and purpose, the reason his sister had to die, his inability to follow his own path." She blinked hard. "I wanted to help him find peace, but I couldn't, not when duty and responsibility weighed so heavily on his soul."

"He was not a strong man," Ramona said in a quiet voice. Before Miriam could lash out at the cruel remark, the other woman held up a hand. "I can say this because I loved an equally weak man. He wanted to be with me, said he'd help raise Cash, but I refused. I had responsibilities to my nephew and this man had a whole world of opportunity waiting for him. Oh, but he had such dreams. How could I tie him down and keep him from achieving those beautiful dreams?" She shrugged, her dark eyes glittering. "I couldn't so I let him go and when he was certain I wouldn't change my mind, he left. It was a horrible time. A few months passed and the pain of missing him wouldn't stop, nor would the memories of him begging me to give 'us' a chance. I started to think he might be right; maybe we *did* belong together. I decided to call and tell him I'd changed my mind." She settled her gaze on the salad bowl and said, "I called but he wasn't home." Her voice dipped so low Miriam had to lean closer to hear. "He was at his engagement party. Seems those words he spouted were recyclable."

"Oh, Ramona, I'm so sorry. I had no idea." Miriam laid a hand on the woman's shoulder, her brain swirling with so many questions, ones she had no right to ask. "I'm so sorry," she said again.

"Thank you."

"You must have really loved him."

She nodded. "I did, even when I learned he was engaged and later, that he'd given up on his dreams for money and power."

"Did you ever see him again?"

Ramona's dark eyes misted. "Sadly, yes. But I didn't recognize him."

The way she said that told Miriam she wasn't talking about the man's physical appearance, but rather, the person inside. "It would have been better if you hadn't seen him."

"Yes, but the wondering wouldn't have stopped. So, is it better to know a truth you'd rather not know, or just keep pretending?" She cleared her throat and unwrapped a piece of Pecorino Romano cheese. "Sometimes you can't pretend anymore, but most people don't like to acknowledge the truth." She grated the cheese on a paper plate, creating a mound that reminded Miriam of the snowdrifts outside. "Not us, though. We look it straight in the eye." Her lips curved into a faint smile. "We're more alike than we care to admit."

Miriam wasn't so sure about that, but there were some similarities. She and Ramona were both strong-minded, independent, loyal, nonconformists. "I guess we do share a few traits."

Ramona nodded, creating another pile of cheese with the grater, while Miriam transferred the first pile into the cheese container using a large serving spoon. "And our one true loves were not our husbands."

"You were married?"

"Oh, yes. A lifetime ago."

"I had no idea."

"There are days I forget that part of my life existed. And then something happens, a word, an item of clothing, the look on a person's face, and it all comes back." She sighed. "The pain, the loss, so fresh and sharp it suffocates me."

Miriam should not ask her to explain. It wasn't her business, not any of it, and yet, she doubted Ramona had spoken about this to anyone in years, if ever. Perhaps it would help to tell someone who wouldn't judge her, who had married a man she ended up detesting. "If you want to talk, you know I'll never repeat what you tell me."

"I know that about you, Miriam. That's another way we're alike." When she started on her third mound of cheese, she also began to talk. "I was twenty when I married. He was much older, with children a year or two younger than me. He promised to take me to Florence and Paris, where we'd sleep on satin sheets, drink champagne, and eat crepes. For a girl from Buffalo, New York, this was a fairy tale. Of course, it never happened."

She paused, sucked in a breath, and pushed on. "He'd built a home in Florida, said it was for me because I was his rose and this was my garden. Imported marble, crystal chandeliers, murals, the greenest lawns you ever saw." She shrugged, stared at the dwindling hunk of cheese in her hand. "What did I know? I believed him." Another pause. "The hitting started two months after we were married when he spotted me talking to one of his business associates at a dinner party. He said the man was a lecher and I was flirting. After, Carlo apologized with a diamond bracelet and three dozen roses, claimed it was the drink that made him crazy. The second time, he broke my nose when he caught me talking to the gardener. He had a great passion for flowers, especially roses, and I wanted to surprise him with a new hybrid. But men who hit their women rarely believe the truth." She touched the bump on her nose. "He was always so remorseful afterward, promised it would never happen again. Until it did. It went on for months and then one day, I learned I was pregnant." She cleared her throat, opened her mouth to speak, but only silence followed.

"I'm so sorry." Nick Desantro had left his own brand of

scars on Miriam, and while they weren't visible, they were deep and painful.

"We were so excited. Carlo became the perfect husband. Oh, but we had plans. He wanted a boy, but I only wished for a healthy child. We called in a designer to help with the nursery... Carlo thought I was having an affair with the man, called me all kinds of horrible names and threatened me. When he grabbed a poker, I ran. I made it to my car and took off." She stopped, blinked hard. "I didn't see the red light; never saw the other car until a second before it hit me..."

Miriam clasped Ramona's hand. "I can't imagine." But in a way, she could. She'd suffered miscarriages and the birth of her daughter, Anna, who only lived a matter of hours.

"I lost the baby, ended up in the hospital with a concussion and a broken collarbone. Carlo left me alone for a few months, but he always had his eye on me. One day he told me he wanted another child and I knew I couldn't do that, to myself or the baby. I waited until he left for his weekly massage, grabbed three hundred dollars from his study, and told the cook I had a hair appointment. I left the car six blocks from the bus stop and found my way here."

"He never came after you?" A man like that did not seem the type to give up what he thought was his.

Ramona shrugged. "He wouldn't have known where to look. Carlo didn't want me to maintain ties with my family and I didn't mind leaving them behind. When I look back, I see how eager I was to pretend I wasn't the product of two alcoholic parents from a less-than-reputable family. I thought money would replace self-esteem and self-worth." She sighed and said in a quiet voice, "How wrong I was."

"What happened to your sister and her husband?" The

ones the town had wondered about since the day they left Cash with Ramona and never returned. Most believed they'd suffered a tragic end. Why else would parents stay away? "Did they die?"

"No, they didn't die, at least not then. I have no idea if they're still alive or where they might be. Teresa and Slim, nickname for Randy, got tired of parenting. Too constricting, they said, not 'fun' enough, and since they'd given me safe harbor, they said I owed them."

So, they'd simply grown tired of parenting. "I'd say Cash was lucky to have you."

"I love that boy as if he were my own. Sometimes, I forget he's not."

"Birthing a child doesn't make a person a parent. It's the day in, day out, being there no matter what, that counts. And that's what you did for Cash, Ramona." Miriam's voice dipped. "You're his real mother."

Ramona's expression softened with Miriam's words. "Thank you for saying that. It means a lot. Enough about me; what else can we do to help Lucy?"

"How about talk to her father and try to make him see this isn't his decision?" Lucy was as strong-willed as her grandmother had been and if Anthony didn't stop pushing, he'd cause more damage to the bruised relationship with his daughter.

Ramona looked away, picked at a piece of dried cheese on the grater. "I tried but I think it only made things worse."

"You talked to Anthony?" Ramona didn't talk to anyone who wasn't a customer or family, and Anthony Benito was neither.

"I did." Pause. "He came to my house." When Ramona met her gaze, Miriam saw the truth in those dark eyes, a truth she was certain this woman had never shared with anyone else. *Anthony Benito was the man Ramona had loved and lost.*

***

For years after, the town would talk about the Christmas Eve a truck carrying snow blowers hit a telephone pole and took out the power, casting Magdalena in complete darkness. No twinkling lights, no sparkling decorations, no trains circling the tree. Nothing but candles and flashlights providing illumination to a town known for its strength and grit, a town that would not be kept down by an inconvenience like the loss of power.

Dusk had just settled in and wiped out the last bits of light from the late afternoon when the truck hit the pole. Harry and Greta Blacksworth's guests covered the first floor, from the living room to the dining room, spilling into the kitchen as they sipped their drinks and munched on canapés, bruschetta, dips and veggies, antipasto, and fresh fruit. The smell of ham blended with the aroma of manicotti and sauce baking in the oven. A Blacksworth gathering was about food and more food, coupled with a good beverage and even better company.

Harry stood near the fire, sipping his scotch and taking it all in. The lights, the laughter, the squeals of the children; it was about friends and family. His friends. His family. When had he ever felt this content? Greta was in the kitchen with Miriam and Ramona, three sergeants in charge of cooking and setting out the meal, which made it awfully difficult to steal a meatball or two. He'd almost held back on inviting Ramona Casherdon to dinner because she wasn't exactly the sociable type, but Pop said she was like calamari, the ones with the tentacles: intimidating until the third bite and then it's a favorite. Doubtful she'd want to be compared to calamari, but Pop did have a point, and besides, who the hell wanted to eat alone on Christmas Eve? He glanced at the overstuffed chair where Pop was holding court, dressed in a candy cane sweater, red corduroys, and a Santa Claus tie. Lucy, Lily, Gina, and Ben clustered around him, all smiles and laughter. The old guy could do that to you, make you think about the good parts of life instead of the rotten ones that tried to seep through like too much balsamic vinegar on a salad.

Too bad Pop's son didn't have his father's disposition. What was his deal anyway? Harry still hadn't forgotten the night the guy strutted into his house as though Pop were an invalid and Lucy a baby and declared they were heading back to California with him. Right, as in not happening. Those were fighting words for Pop, and Lucy wasn't far behind in her feistiness. Tony had been no match for the two of them, as he learned that night. Now the guy stood next to the Christmas tree, sipping his drink, studying the ornaments as if he'd never seen handmade decorations before. Come to think of it, maybe he hadn't. Huh. He did seem intrigued by the construction paper chains and popcorn garland, though not as much as the dough handprints with the pictures of AJ, Lizzie, Jackson, and Lily on them. Harry had been pretty amazed several weeks ago when he came home and found Greta making decorations with the kids. The thought made his chest ache with remembering. Maybe he'd wander over and see if he could get Tony to loosen up a bit and enjoy the festivities instead of sulking because his father and daughter were staying in Magdalena. Though, if Harry were a betting man, he'd say the guy had bigger issues, and he'd guess the issues started and ended with Tony Benito and his how-can-this-be-my-life mantra.

Harry started to make his way toward Tony when the power went out, accompanied by a succession of buzzes, beeps, and dings. The only light in the room came from the fireplace and that was nothing compared to the wattage he'd had flowing through the house seconds ago. "What the hell happened?" Chatter filled the room, followed by a commotion of movement toward the light from the fireplace. What now? "Nate! Where are you?" If anybody could figure out why the power went out, it was Nate.

Someone whistled and the chatter died. "Take it easy." Nate's deep voice reached Harry from across the room. "We'll figure this out, but you have to stay calm. Cash, light the fireplaces on the first floor. AJ, ask your mother where the flashlights are and bring one to me. I want everybody in this room. Ben, call Rudy Dean and see if he knows what's going on. Harry and Tony, come with me."

"What do you plan to do?" This from Tony.

"We're going to rearrange the furniture so we're closer together."

"Shouldn't we just go home?" Tony Benito asked.

Harry didn't need extra light to tell Nate didn't like the question, and sure enough when the boy spoke, his words were slathered with ticked-off annoyance. "Nobody's leaving until we know the status of the rest of the town. If there's no power, that probably means no heat." He tossed a look in Harry's direction and added, "Unless they've got a generator, which we don't."

Nate was never going to give up on that damn generator story. Harry had intended to order it from the information Nate gave him, even had the specs sitting next to the phone. But then he got sidetracked by the selection of ties and matching socks in the new clothing catalog he favored, and well, what could he say? Clothing accessories beat out a clunky machine. It's not like Nate had said Harry absolutely *had* to have it this winter, as in immediately; he'd called it the best security blanket money could buy. Okay, but money could buy it next season, too, right? Only problem was, Harry needed it *this* season, like right this second.

Before Nate could make another comment about the lack of a generator, Ben Reed spoke up. "I just got off the phone with the chief and the whole town's out. Seems a truck hit a telephone pole on Elderberry Road. No idea how long it'll be out, but he said to stay off the roads."

"So it looks like we're camping out here tonight, Harry." Cash laid a hand on his shoulder and said, "One big sleepover, just what you wanted."

"We're stuck?" Tony Benito made his way to Nate, disbelief coating his words. "That's it? Can't we at least try to get out of here so we can sleep in our own beds?"

Ben Reed stepped forward and said, "Did you hear what I just said? The power's out all over town and the police chief wants people to stay put, and that means us."

Tony was not going to let it go. "But surely you've been without power before. What are a few extra blankets piled on a bed to keep you warm? And Pop has a gas stove so we can cook, too. Frankly, I think we should all head home and hunker down in our own places."

Cash Casherdon muttered something under his breath and said, "Well, *frankly*, nobody asked you. If the police chief says stay put, we're staying put."

"Listen to these boys, Tony. They'll keep us safe." Pop's voice was gentle, but Harry doubted his son would appreciate a public put-down. Couldn't the guy see that these men geared up for challenges that threatened their families and excelled at overcoming them? Harry would take Nate, Cash, and Ben to protect him any day, in any situation. Tony was trying to take control of something he didn't understand and looking like ten kinds of a fool. Harry knew better than to start spouting off solutions; he preferred playing host and following instructions. A man had to know his limitations and a good bottle of bourbon could forgive a lot—like neglecting to order a generator.

"You sound like I did when I first moved here," Harry said, intent on diffusing the situation with a half truth. "I wanted to get things done fast, pay whoever I needed to in order to get the job done, and forget about waiting for anything, especially people or nature. But I learned fast that I wasn't first in command." He laughed and shook his head. "I wasn't even second or third, and the best I could do was relax and trust the people who were."

This seemed to appease Tony because he shoved his hands in his pockets and said, "I'm not used to sitting around and waiting for things to happen. I'm usually the one *making* them happen."

"Good." Harry said. "Did you hear that, Nate? Tony's one of your go-to men, so keep him included in the plans." Massaging a guy's ego always pumped him up, made him *want* to pitch in.

Nate turned toward Harry, rubbed the back of his neck, and said, "Right."

That could mean anything with Nate, but it was better to leave it alone and not ask for clarification.

"What about our presents?" Lily's voice swirled around the room. "I made them special, and I've been waiting forever to hand them out."

"I don't know, Lily." Nate's voice turned soft as he talked to his sister. "Right now I want to make sure everybody stays warm, and then make sure they have food to eat, and maybe we'll see about presents."

"Okay," she said, but Harry didn't miss the tremble of disappointment in her voice. The child wasn't asking to open a present, damn, but she wanted to *give* a present. If that didn't represent love and giving, he didn't know what did.

Harry could not stand that sadness in her voice and tossed out a salve, intent on making her feel better. "We'll get it done, Lily girl. All of it, and then you can hand out your presents."

"Right." This from Nate again, one word, loaded with a warning for Harry to stop making promises he might not be able to keep. Nate was right, of course, but damn, it was hard to disappoint a kid.

Lily clapped her hands and said, "Thank you, Uncle Harry."

"Yes!" Lizzie copied Lily with the hand-clapping. "Thank you, Mr. Harry!"

"Welcome," Harry muttered, dreading the second Greta got him alone and began the lecture about responsible parenting and not giving in to whims. It was coming, like a white Christmas in Magdalena, and there was no way to avoid it.

Chapter 8

Pop would never forget this Christmas Eve, not if he lived another ten months or ten years, unless he really did get the Alzheimer's his son had been so worried about. Who could ask for more than friends and family coming together despite half-cooked manicotti, cold meatballs, a ham and green bean casserole cooked on the grill, and marshmallows toasted in three separate fireplaces? Maybe they didn't eat off the fancy china, but what was wrong with a paper plate? Some of Pop's best meals had been eaten on them. Okay, so they'd needed to double up on the plates so the sauce didn't seep through, but nobody seemed to care. Heck, nobody seemed to notice. Once the boys got the fires going and the furniture rearranged, couches and chairs scooted in from other rooms and pulled into a big circle, they were all set.

Nate Desantro even played Christmas carols on the piano as his wife and baby sat beside him, while Lily and Lizzie danced. Pop did a jig with them, too. Never too old for a dance with a pretty girl or two is what he always said. Harry Blacksworth must have thought the same thing because once Lizzie got him moving, the man twirled, dipped, and taught Lily to waltz. It was a sight to see and Pop had to blink hard a time or two before the dang emotions took over and spilled a tear. The teary eyes happened again when Ben Reed slow-danced with his new bride, circling the tiny spot of floor, his arms holding her close, her head resting on his strong chest. The sight reminded Pop of the dance they shared at Tess and Cash's wedding, minus the baby and the love they'd added. Ah, but it was something to witness such love and devotion. He and Lucy had been the same way and only someone who's never known that kind of love can say it dies with the person. Not true. That kind of love lives and breathes until the other half takes one final breath and joins his soul mate. And that's what Ben and Gina Reed shared, and Nate and Christine Desantro, and Cash and Tess Casherdon. Harry and Greta Blacksworth, too. But not Brody and Bree Kinkaid, and certainly not Tony and his ex-wife.

Maybe one day Lucy would find her soul mate and then she'd know, too. And maybe Tony would have a second chance at finding happiness with the right person, but before that happened, the boy had to take a long look at the road he was on and see where he was headed. If he didn't like the direction, he'd better darn well change it or he'd end somewhere he didn't want to be. Like miserable. Speaking of miserable, had he seen Ramona Casherdon almost smiling? Why, he could have sworn he had, right about the time Nate started playing "Jingle Bells" and Harry serenaded them with a few lines. The woman was a looker when she smiled and relaxed the frown lines around her mouth and eyes. Yes, indeed she was. He'd have to congratulate Harry for including Ramona in the Christmas Eve dinner. Sitting on the outside of life was a dang lonely place to be, even if a person said that's where he wanted to be and made sure everybody knew it. After a while, people believed the words, even if they weren't true, and the person who said them got caught in his own trap. And what's that get him but hour after hour of aloneness that eventually twists and churns into a black hole of loneliness. Maybe Ramona was on her way out of that hole, and maybe she'd found a friend in Miriam Desantro to help pull her out.

Harry said they'd been cooking and prepping together

most of the day and Pop had spotted them talking a while ago. A good sign, but not surprising; they were strong women, hard workers, great cooks. Pop would bet his prize basil supply the cooking was what brought them together, but he'd guess heartache had something to do with it as well. Miriam had lost a child, a husband, and Charlie Blacksworth. Ramona hadn't lost a child or a husband so far as Pop knew, and she'd never been seen with a man, but heartache was written on the sternness of her face and the clipped words that spilled from those lips when she did choose to talk. But heartache from what? The sister and brother-in-law who dumped Cash and took off? The husband and child she never had? Nobody really knew Ramona Casherdon and that's exactly the way she liked it. Oh, but he hoped Cash and Tess would have a baby soon, whether their own, adopted, or fostered didn't matter, but it sure would do them all a world of good.

Had he seen Ramona hand Lucy a piece of pumpkin roll just now? Pop sat up in his overstuffed chair and leaned forward, squinting to get a better look. *Dang*, but the woman had given his granddaughter not one, but *two* slices of pumpkin roll! How about that? Ramona was softening up. Pop smiled and watched Lucy munch on the pumpkin roll as Ramona pointed to it like she was giving instructions and making recommendations, which she probably was. A good cook and baker was never 100 percent satisfied with their product; he knew that from his pizzelle making. Watching Lucy scarf the pumpkin roll made him hungry for his own piece. Pop patted his belly, eased out of the chair, and made his way into the dining room. There was a fireplace in this room, too, so he didn't need one of the flashlights AJ had found. Oh, but there was a lot of food here, enough to add an extra pound or two around his middle if he just went for the sweets, or pretended he hadn't eaten an hour ago and started all over again. If his Lucy were here to see this, she'd have a thing or three to say about his food choices. As Pop worked his way around the table, forking two meatballs, a hunk of ham, and a slice of pumpkin roll, he thought of something that would disturb his wife even more, tear her up like a hot pepper sandwich—the sad and lonely look on their son's face tonight, like he didn't belong here, or anywhere.

***

Anthony stared out the window at the snow, mounds of it, some fresh, some tromped on, rolled into snowmen or forts. There'd been a time when he'd loved snow, loved watching his breath come out in puffs of cold. But that was a lifetime ago, and right now, Anthony wished he could have that lifetime back.

The people in this house belonged. They were not outsiders like he was. Even Ben Reed, the newest addition to Magdalena, fell into the group with ease and camaraderie, like he really wanted to be here. Maybe it was the pregnant wife or the friends, or maybe it was the man's ability to blend and give. And what about Cash? He'd left town with a grievous offense pinned to his back, so dark it seemed he'd never lift the weight of it, and yet, not only had he returned, but he'd been welcomed *and* he got the girl. Go figure. A person had to have real heart and forgiveness in their soul to get through what that boy did.

In a few days, Anthony would head back to California, resume his old life, minus a child and a wife. There would be no father to fill up his time with stories and doctor appointments. He'd be alone in a house cramped with lukewarm memories of family life. Oh, he could search out his business associates whom he considered "friends" in the broadest of terms, but after the pleasantries and surface "shop talk," what then? They didn't care about him any more than he cared about them. Nobody would look at him the way people in this town looked at or looked up to his father. And they certainly weren't going to stand up for Anthony if someone attempted to barrel in and take over like he'd tried to do with Pop. There'd be no Nate or Lily Desantro coming to his rescue, no Harry Blacksworth throwing back shots and telling him what a great man he was. There certainly wouldn't be a woman like Ramona Casherdon, warning him in a bold and no-nonsense fashion that he was in danger of losing his relationship with his daughter.

People cared about Pop and now they cared about Lucy. But who cared about him? Anyone? No one? Maybe he would always be an outsider no matter where he went. He stared at the snow. Pure. Mesmerizing. A beacon of redemption, lit by a sliver of moon. Before he stopped to consider the reasons for his actions or the wisdom of them, he flicked on his flashlight and made his way to the back hallway where he yanked on his jacket and hat. *Damn*, but he should have worn boots. He eyed a large pair, Nate Desantro's no doubt. Anthony slipped out of his loafers, pulled on the boots, and tied the laces. When he opened the door, a rush of cold air slapped his face. Snow glistened from the ground, offering up bits of illumination as he clomped down the stairs.

The faint strains of piano chords blended with "O Come All Ye Faithful" reached him from the house. How did this group find joy in their circumstances despite no power, no feast, and no way to make it to their own beds tonight? Weren't they annoyed? Why hadn't they complained, other than to voice their disappointment that they couldn't sample the manicotti? Not a peep from the pregnant woman, Gina Reed, or her husband, Ben, who made it his mission to see to his wife's comfort: a pillow, shoulder rub, extra blanket, cup of fruit, and lots of handholding. Anthony had never acted that way when Rosalyn was pregnant with Lucy, but would his ex-wife have wanted it? Or rather, *permitted* it? Probably not. Anthony supposed if he had to be stuck in a stranded location, having Nate Desantro in charge wasn't a bad thing either.

"Mr. Anthony? Why are you out here all by yourself?"

Anthony turned to find Lily Desantro a few feet behind him, bundled up like a snowman. "Lily. What are you doing out here?"

"I looked out the window and saw you." She moved closer. "You looked like you didn't know what to do." She paused. "Do you want to make an angel?"

"An angel?" He'd avoided direct conversations with the child because she made him uncomfortable. There was something about her that saw through the layers of niceties and got right to the core of the issue. How did she do it? She couldn't possibly know what she was doing and yet he'd witnessed it more than once—from her comments to Lucy about the baby who was going to need a lot of love, to Pop about the car he might want to hand over to Lucy, to Harry and the one or two lessons he needed to learn for when the power went out. The child zeroed in on a pain, addressed it, and moved on, leaving the other person to ponder and evaluate.

"So, do you want me to show you how to make an angel?" She smiled at him, a big smile that spread across her small face. "Daddy said there weren't enough on this earth and we could always use more."

Daddy? She meant Christine Desantro's father, Harry

Blacksworth's brother. Miriam told him the truth the other day, not that she was hiding it, but she wasn't the type to reveal secrets either, unless required. Not that it was exactly a secret, but the man had been married, and apparently the daughter hadn't known about Miriam or Lily. If he'd looked at Lily closer, he would have tied together the unique blue eyes and black hair and marked her a Blacksworth. But he hadn't looked, and now she wanted to teach him to make angels? He shrugged and said, "Sure. Teach me to make an angel."

Lily dropped to her knees, then rolled onto her back, arms stretched, a smile on her face. "You move your arms and legs back and forth, real wide, like this—" she demonstrated the motion with her arms and legs, spreading them in a great arc in the snow "—and that's how you make an angel. Now, you try."

Anthony knelt and rolled onto his back, facing the night sky. As he moved his arms and legs, Lily clapped and let out a small squeal. "You did it, Mr. Anthony. You made a perfect angel." Pause. "Mr. Anthony?"

"Yes?"

"Are you sad that you don't live closer to Pop?"

Had she heard someone talking about how he wanted to take Pop back with him? "Why do you ask?" If he knew her angle, he'd know how to answer the question.

"Because you hardly ever get to see him." Her voice dipped. "You must live really, really far away."

A plane ride. And not a long one either. Guilt pinged him but he pushed it away. "It *is* far," he said. "And Pop doesn't like to visit."

"And you don't like to visit either, do you, Mr. Anthony?"

"Huh?" Who told her that? Had she overheard a

conversation?

"You don't like to visit because it's really, really far away and then you miss your home."

"Right." The home that didn't feel like a home at all, but a structure of beams and glass and marble. A place to sleep, shower, change clothes, and have an occasional meal.

"Yeah, and you miss all of your friends, too."

Friends. He bet Lily Desantro's definition of friends was a lot different from his.

She blew out a soft sigh and lifted a mittened hand in the air. "Hi, Daddy. This is Mr. Anthony. He's my friend, Pop's son. We're making angels. Did you see we lost the power and everything went black?" She giggled. "Nate got a frowny face when he found out Uncle Harry forgot to order the machine that gives you heat and works the oven. Nate said Uncle Harry was too busy matching his socks and ties to remember." Giggle, giggle. "I like Uncle Harry's socks and ties. He has purple with blue…and pink and green…" she went on and on in a sing-song voice, talking to a dead Charles Blacksworth.

No wonder Lily got along so well with Pop; they both talked to dead people like they were sitting next to them.

"Mr. Anthony lives in California and that's really, really far away and he hardly ever gets to see his father. Isn't that sad?" She sniffed. "And now his daughter is going to have a baby and she's staying here, so he probably won't get to see her either. Or the baby. We'll have to send him pictures, because if we don't, the baby will grow up and he won't know what she looks like." Her voice turned gentle. "I think it's a girl, but Pop says it's a boy. He only says that because he wants the boy to look like Mr. Anthony did when he was a baby." She giggled. "Pop says a child is like a flower and you have to take very special care of it so it will bloom." She giggled again. "Kids don't bloom, do they, Daddy?"

Lily's words pierced his heart, made it bleed. He tried to block out her voice, but it slithered through him, showing him what he'd refused to see. "I miss you, Daddy." Her voice wobbled. "Miss you so much. Mr. Anthony's lucky, isn't he, Daddy? He can see his father and his daughter and his grandbaby all at the same time. Lucky, lucky, lucky."

***

It was after midnight when everyone settled down; couples snuggled in blankets on couches, sleeping bags, and mountains of pillows. Bodies paired up like matching socks. Pop insisted on the overstuffed chair but permitted Miriam to slide the ottoman under his legs. Harry's three kids and Lily had crawled into sleeping bags, lined side by side. Nate and Christine Desantro slept on a couch, their baby in a pop-up playpen next to them. And the pregnant Reeds shared another couch, the handsome husband's hand resting on his wife's belly. The Blacksworths slept in a recliner, Harry's head turned to the side, Greta's resting on his shoulder. He'd have a damned stiff neck in the morning, but Anthony guessed he wouldn't complain; maybe the guy wouldn't even notice. Lucy, Ramona, and Miriam slept on another couch, longer and wider than the other ones, a beautiful cream leather with wide stitching. Designer quality, certainly not sleepover material. But Blacksworth didn't seem to care. He'd laughed and said he only bought it because the color reminded him of his wife's complexion.

What did a person say to that? Anthony had never thought of purchasing anything because it reminded him of Rosalyn, not even her diamond ring, which she'd preselected to ensure she got exactly what she wanted. He wondered if she did get what she wanted: the lifestyle, the marriage, the child? She might have done without the last, though he'd never breathe that truth out loud.

He made his way to the dining room, away from the sleeping crowd. The empty recliner next to Pop was meant for him, but Anthony couldn't sleep, not yet, with Lily Desantro's excitement over her gift-giving so fresh in his brain. Pressed flowers in frames with words like *joy, love, hope,* scrawled above them for her "family." But that family didn't just include blood relatives, it extended to Pop, the Reeds, and the Casherdons.

"Dad?" He turned to find Lucy standing next to him, a blanket flung over her shoulders, her body illuminated by the glow of the dining room fireplace.

"Lucy. Why are you still awake?"

"I couldn't sleep."

"Me either."

She gestured toward the doorway that led to the kitchen. "Are you hungry? I could make you a ham sandwich."

He smiled. Food, the making of it, the sharing and eating of it, that was this town's answer to catastrophes, natural and manmade. It had been this way when he was a boy and his mother sent him to Mrs. Mulldaney's with fresh baked bread when her seventh child entered the world. And the year Arthur Lane broke his leg and was out of work for three months, didn't the town send his family meals, and a birthday cake for his youngest? "I'm fine, but thank you."

She bit her lower lip, shifting from one foot to the other and said, "How about a slice of pumpkin roll? It's really good, not like store bought. There's at least two inches of cream cheese mix in the roll." She paused. "I had three slices."

His gaze darted to her belly, then back to her face. "Three, huh?"

Her lips twitched and she said, "It has nothing to do with the baby. I love anything pumpkin."

He'd thought she loved anything chocolate. "Good to know." He tried to make out her expression but the fire cast a shadow over her face, making it difficult.

"I'm sorry I've been such a disappointment to you," she blurted out. "You must really hate me right now."

"Don't say that." He touched her shoulder. "You're my daughter. I love you." Didn't she know that? Couldn't she tell that despite his screwed-up parenting skills, he loved her? Would always love her? She sniffed and shrugged. "I'm the one who's sorry," he said. "I should have been there for you, but I got so caught up in work and what I thought I should be doing for my family that I forgot about the people *in* that family." He tucked a lock of hair behind her ear, stroked her cheek. "I lost my way."

She nodded. "I used to wish I was Julia's daughter because then I'd have brothers and sisters and a father who came home every night."

Lucy wanted to be the cook's daughter? How sad that she'd wanted to be a servant's child rather than his and Rosalyn's. "I think I'm the one who should be apologizing." He'd made years of wrong choices. Where did he begin to try and change so he could make things right? Was it even possible?

"I'm not going back to school." She paused, went on, "I mean not my old school. I'll sign up at the community college."

There was the faintest hint of defiance in her words, possibly in preparation for battle—with him. Anthony nodded. "Okay." He didn't want to fight and tear down; he wanted to rebuild.

She pulled the blanket tighter around her. "And I'm staying in Magdalena."

"I know." One word at a time.

"With Grandpa."

"With Grandpa," he repeated. Maybe Pop could teach them both a thing or two about relationships.

"Dad?"

"Huh?" He'd been thinking about Pop and how he owed him an apology.

"His name was Gray, short for Grayson." Her voice dipped, pinged his heart. "I thought he loved me...but he just...he just..."

"It's okay, sweetheart." He pulled her into his arms, stroked her back, and whispered, "It's okay."

"I should have known better," she murmured against his chest. "I *did* know better, but I listened to him. When I told him I was pregnant, he said it could have been any guy, even though he knew it wasn't."

Bastard. Stay calm, stay calm. "So this Grayson won't be in your life or the baby's?"

She shook her head. "No."

"Good," he said. He was beginning to realize that blood didn't make families; they were made by people who cared, and gave, and loved.

Lucy lifted her head and eased away so she could look at him. "Will you come back when the baby's born? The doctor thinks it will be the middle of April."

Anthony smiled at his daughter, the first real smile in months and said, "I'll be here. You can count on it."

Chapter 9

The power came on early Christmas morning and the story told for years after said Old Saint Nick had a lot to do with it. How else did a body explain the mountain of presents under the tree in the living room? They'd all slept in that room last night, in awful darn close quarters, and no one had heard a peep, not a single footstep or rustle of paper. But when the lights blinked on and the buzzers and dings startled them awake at 5:52 a.m., there were presents under that tree for every one of them, presents that had not been there when they fell asleep. Not just a pair of socks either, but handpicked-for-the-person gifts. Now that took a lot of thought and there were those like Nate Desantro, his mother, and Ramona Casherdon, who wouldn't write a Christmas wish list if someone offered them the lottery. And the thing was, the gifts weren't ones they might ask for, but if you thought about it a bit, they were a perfect fit. A custom blend of specialty meat seasonings for Nate, a pair of handcrafted earrings for Miriam and a matching bracelet designed by an artist in Philly. A royal blue shawl for Ramona, not the dang black she favored like a mourner. Pop couldn't wait to get home and try out his brand-new pizzelle maker. When Tony opened his gift, Pop thought it might annoy him more than anything else. It was a navy and green scarf, pricey from the looks of it, but intended for snow, no doubt about that, which might be a subtle suggestion to stick around Magdalena or, at least, visit more often. Tony had made no bones about getting out of this place, but the boy didn't look annoyed, not one bit. He stared at that scarf and then he smiled, like he was actually happy. Well, if that didn't beat all.

Pop would let the rest of them wonder about those gifts and the giver, but he had an idea who'd been playing Old Saint Nick, yes, indeed he did. The giver had a heart as big as a Christmas turkey and a sense of style, too, and his first name was Harry.

It was early afternoon by the time they all made it out of the Blacksworths' home, bellies full, hearts content. Tony had a flight out tomorrow, though he hadn't mentioned a word about Pop or Lucy staying behind. That would come soon enough and if it didn't, Pop would have to bring it up. The boy had never liked defeat or disappointment, especially when they were attached to family. Maybe that's why he'd avoided coming home for so many years; didn't have to look in the mirror and see how far he'd strayed. Who knew what was in Tony's head? Pop had caught him talking to Lucy this morning, even laughing a time or two, and dang if he didn't place a hand on his daughter's belly. Now that said something, but Pop wasn't sure what or how much. But he'd find out before his son hopped on that plane tomorrow, oh, yes, indeed he would.

"Hey, Dad, got a minute?"

Pop looked up from his new pizzelle maker. He had a hankering to make a batch and he'd see if Lucy wanted to help him. A body never could get too much practice in the art of pizzelle making. But the look on Tony's face said he had something on his mind and he had to get it off before it burrowed a hole straight through. "Sure. Have a seat." Tony plunked down in the chair next to Pop, facing the portrait of Lucinda Benito. Nothing came out of his mouth, though, not a whisper and that's when Pop knew his son needed an intervention. "Just spit it out, Tony. No need to play fancy with me. I'm guessing you're going to give it one more go and work on convincing me to get on that plane with you tomorrow. Lucy, too. Never mind the cost or the inconvenience, or the plain fact that we don't want to go—"

"I want you and Lucy to stay here."

Pop scratched his jaw, leaned toward his son. "Did I hear you right? You *want* me and Lucy to stay in Magdalena?"

Tony dragged his gaze to Pop's. "It's where you belong, I see that now. These people care about you and they care about Lucy, too." He shrugged, his dark eyes bright. "I can't compete with that." His voice dipped, turned sad. "I wouldn't even know how."

Pop patted his son's hand. "This ain't no competition, Tony. You're my son, my number one, and don't forget that. I don't want to go to California because this is my home; it's where I've lived most of my life, and it's where I want to take my last breath. Doesn't make it right, doesn't make it wrong. Lucy will find that out soon enough. She's got a baby on the way, no husband, no education, and no job. So, for now, we'll try to guide her along as best we can, make her feel safe, and help her out, but she's got to grow up. She'll learn that fast once the baby comes."

"I wish I'd been a better parent."

"We all wish we'd been better parents, but we do the best we can and when we make a mistake, we own up to it, and try again."

Tony's expression relaxed. "I talked to Lucy last night. It felt good."

Pop smiled and nodded. "That's a start."

"You don't think it's too late for us?" The worry crept back into his voice, slithered across his words.

"It's only too late when you close your eyes for the last time. The girl loves you, Tony." He paused, zeroed in on his son's face, and said, "I love you, too."

Tony cleared his throat twice and said, "I love you, too, Dad. I'm coming back when the baby's born, and maybe one time before that."

"So, you're gonna take the grandpa duties seriously, huh?"

"I think I better work on the father duties first. Maybe you could give me a crash course?"

Pop slid a quick glance at the portrait of his wife and could have sworn her eyes twinkled. *He's finally come back to us, Lucy. All these years and our boy has come home to his roots.* "If you're ready to learn, I'm ready to teach. Lesson number one is what I call 'The art of making the perfect pizzelle.' Master this and you'll have mastered patience, charity, perseverance, and above all, love."

***

Anthony pulled out of his father's driveway the next morning, the small box of pizzelles they'd made yesterday resting on the front seat. He'd dreaded coming to Magdalena and now that it was time to leave, he wasn't ready, not after he'd just begun a relationship with the two most important people in his world—his father and his daughter. When he mentioned he wouldn't mind staying on a few more weeks, Pop told him to get on that plane back to California and think about what he wanted, and then figure out how to get it. His father even gave him the talk about how the really valuable gifts in life couldn't be bought, and this time, Anthony understood. He *did* have a lot to think about and right now he had no idea what direction to take, but with enough time and what Pop called "searching his gut and his soul," he might just figure it out.

Fresh snow had fallen last night, prompting Anthony to allow extra time for the airport trip. But the snow wasn't the only reason for his early departure. He had one last stop to make before he left town. Twenty-eight years was a long time to hold something inside, but he owed Ramona that much. When she opened the door, he was twenty-five again, taken in by the beauty and mystery of the woman.

"Hello, Tony."

The huskiness in her voice pulled him in, made him stumble over his words. "I...do you have a minute?" She opened the door and he brushed past her, the faint smell of powdered sugar filling him. "I'm on my way to the airport but I wanted to stop here first."

Her dark eyes narrowed on him. "Another good-bye?"

"Yes." He shook his head. "No. I'm leaving, but I'll be back."

A spark of emotion flickered across her face, then disappeared. "And what does that have to do with me?" She crossed her arms over her middle like a shield.

"Nothing." Pause. "Unless you want it to. I have totally screwed up my life. Married the wrong person, spent years chasing the wrong things, attached value to nothing." He cleared his throat, continued. "I don't want to be that person anymore. I haven't liked him in a long time. I've got a lot to fix, and I'm working on making things better with my dad and my daughter." He moved toward her, clasped her shoulders. "I have never loved anyone the way I loved you." His voice shifted, grew hoarse. "The way I still love you." There. He'd said it.

She didn't look impressed or moved to make a similar confession. Instead, her dark brows pinched together and her lips pulled into a straight line. What had he expected from her? A profession of love and forgiveness? Anthony pushed past his disappointment and continued. "I am so very sorry for the pain I caused you, and I will spend the rest of my life regretting my actions and my foolishness." Ramona stared at him, eyes bright, mouth clamped shut, and Anthony saw the truth. It was too late; it had been too late the second he gave up on them twenty-eight years ago. He released her and placed a soft kiss on her forehead. "Good-bye, Ramona. Be well."

He made it to the front door.

"I don't know what you want from me, Tony."

He turned to see the pain and anguish on her face, maybe even a bit of fear. His heart swelled with equal amounts of sadness and hope. "Only what you can give, but not until I've earned it." He stayed near the door, his hand on the knob. "I've got a long way to go to earn your trust, I know that."

She swiped at her face, impatience coating her next words. "But why, Tony? I'm not that same woman I was all those years ago. I'm old and frayed at the edges, and I'm surprised you can't see that."

"I don't see that, not at all." He moved toward her, stopped when he was a foot away, and touched the gold hoop in her left ear. "I see the woman I love, the one I'm hoping will give me a second chance."

"But Tony—"

He placed a finger against her lips. "Let me show you, not with fancy words like I once did, but with actions that speak of commitment and love. I've got some things to sort out, but I'm coming back to Magdalena, maybe to stay or just visit." He traced her jaw. "Or maybe I'll keep a place here and travel, and maybe you'll come with me."

The brilliance of her smile pulled him in, held him, and then she said, "Maybe I will."

The End

Many thanks for choosing to spend your time reading *A Family Affair: Christmas*. I'm truly grateful. If you enjoyed it, please consider writing a review on the site where you purchased it. (Short ones are fine and equally welcome.)

If you'd like to be notified of my new releases, please sign up at my website: *http://www.marycampisi.com*.

What's Next

I love creating secondary characters—they can be so complicated and yet so very intriguing. I've often wondered how they'd react if they were given the opportunity for their own story.

Well, the opportunity has arrived!

I plan to introduce people from That Second Chance Series to *A Family Affair's* Magdalena, New York, starting with *Simple Riches'* "Bad Boy," Michael Androvich and "Good Girl," Elise Pentani. They'll both appear in *A Family Affair: Winter*, which is not going to make them one bit happy, seeing as they'd rather live in different universes than spend another minute in the same town. I guess that's what happens when a person gets left at the altar... (Not saying which one, but it's going to be brutal and humiliating.) I can't wait for the residents of Magdalena to meet these two and see if they can help heal two broken hearts. With Lily's curiosity and Pop's matchmaking endeavors, it will be quite interesting...

Note: The following characters from That Second Chance Series will appear in future *A Family Affair* books, though not necessarily in the order listed:

Grant Richot (*Pulling Home*, That Second Chance Series, Book One)

Angie Sorrento (*The Way They Were*, That Second Chance Series, Book Two)

Adam Brandon (*Paradise Found*, That Second Chance Series Book Four)

See you in Magdalena!

About the Author

Mary Campisi writes emotion-packed books about second chances. Whether contemporary romances, women's fiction, or Regency historicals, her books all center on belief in the beauty of that second chance. Mary should have known she'd become a writer when at age thirteen she began changing the ending to all the books she read. It took several years and a number of jobs, including registered nurse, receptionist in a swanky hair salon, accounts payable clerk, and practice manager in an OB/GYN office, for her to rediscover writing. Enter a mouse-less computer, a floppy disk, and a dream large enough to fill a zip drive. The rest of the story lives on in every book she writes.

When she's not working on her craft or following the lives of five adult children, Mary's digging in the dirt with her flowers and herbs, cooking, reading, walking her rescue lab mix, Cooper, or on the perfect day, riding off into the sunset with her very own 'hero' husband on his Ultra Limited aka Harley.

Mary has published with Kensington, Carina Press, and The Wild Rose Press. She is currently working on her next A Family Affair book as the saga continues…

website: www.marycampisi.com
e-mail: mary@marycampisi.com
twitter: https://twitter.com/#!/MaryCampisi
blog: http://www.marycampisi.com/blog/
facebook: http://www.facebook.com/marycampisibooks

Other Books by Mary Campisi:

Contemporary Romance:

Truth in Lies Series
Book One: A Family Affair
Book Two: A Family Affair: Spring
Book Three: A Family Affair: Summer
Book Four: A Family Affair: Fall
Book Five: A Family Affair: Christmas
Book Six: A Family Affair: Winter (2015)
Book Seven: A Family Affair: ... (TBA)

That Second Chance Series
Book One: Pulling Home
Book Two: The Way They Were
Book Three: Simple Riches
Book Four: Paradise Found
Book Five: Not Your Everyday Housewife
Book Six: The Butterfly Garden

The Betrayed Trilogy
Book One: Pieces of You
Book Two: Secrets of You
Book Three: What's Left of Her: a novella
The Betrayed Trilogy Boxed Set

Single Titles:
Begin Again: Short stories from the heart
The Sweetest Deal

Regency Historical: